New York Bachelors' Club

Time to change their minds?

Through thick and thin, Dr. Kaleb Sabat and
Dr. Snowden Tangredi have *always* had each other's
backs. So, when life—or, rather, love!—hits them
hard, they make a vow. No more relationships!

But just as soon as they promise to be lifelong
bachelors, two *incredible* women arrive at their
hospital…ready to rewrite the New York
bachelors' rules!

Meet the staff of
New York Memorial Hospital with…

Kaleb and Nicola's Story
Consequences of Their New York Night

Snowden and Kirsten's Story
The Trouble with the Tempting Doc

Available now!

Dear Reader,

Have you ever felt like you misjudged someone and weren't sure what to do about it? Or have you ever doubted your ability to read people correctly? That's the case with plastic surgeon Kaleb Sabat. He's had two relationships—both of which ended badly—and decides that love must be meant for someone other than him. So one night, he and his best friend toast to failed relationships and make a bachelor's pact: they're both staying single. Permanently.

Except those kinds of resolutions rarely take. And it's no different for Kaleb. Because the evening of his bachelor pact, he has a one-night stand. With a beautiful pulmonologist. And it changes everything.

Thank you for joining Kaleb and Nicola as they face some hard realities neither of them is ready for. But fate has a funny way of using those times to give you just what you need. This special couple is about to find that out. I hope you love reading their story as much as I loved writing it!

Love,

Tina Beckett

CONSEQUENCES
OF THEIR
NEW YORK NIGHT

———

TINA BECKETT

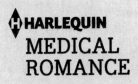

HARLEQUIN
MEDICAL
ROMANCE

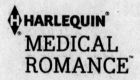

HARLEQUIN®
MEDICAL ROMANCE™

Recycling programs for this product may not exist in your area.

ISBN-13: 978-1-335-40440-4

Consequences of Their New York Night

Copyright © 2021 by Tina Beckett

This edition published by arrangement with Harlequin Books S.A.

For questions and comments about the quality of this book, please contact us at CustomerService@Harlequin.com.

Harlequin Enterprises ULC
22 Adelaide St. West, 40th Floor
Toronto, Ontario M5H 4E3, Canada
www.Harlequin.com

Printed in U.S.A.

Three-times Golden Heart® Award finalist **Tina Beckett** learned to pack her suitcases almost before she learned to read. Born to a military family, she has lived in the United States, Puerto Rico, Portugal and Brazil. In addition to traveling, Tina loves to cuddle with her pug, Alex, spend time with her family and hit the trails on her horse. Learn more about Tina from her website, or friend her on Facebook.

Visit the Author Profile page
at Harlequin.com for more titles.

For my husband. Always and forever.

PROLOGUE

KALEB SABAT THUMPED a glass of whiskey in front of his friend without saying a word. The bar was packed with the normal weekend crowd. Singles trolling for some easy company for the night. People celebrating the wins and losses they'd experienced during the day. Kaleb was there for none of those things.

He'd been the best man at his buddy's wedding five years ago, just as they were both finishing up medical school. And now he was here drinking to the finalizing of Snowden's divorce. It wasn't exactly a celebration, but close enough. Kaleb could only be glad he and his fiancée had called it quits before it got to the point of selling a home and dividing up assets.

"Hell," Snow said, then tipped back his glass and drained it in two swallows. "Why did we have to be so young and stupid, anyway? First your relationship crashes. And then mine."

"I have no idea." He took a drink of his own whiskey and gave a slight grimace as the brew bit the back of his throat and traced a path of fire down his esophagus. A good kind of fire.

Friends since the time they were kids, Snow had spent more time at Kaleb's house than he had at his own as they were growing up. Only later did Kaleb find out why. His friend's home hadn't been a very good example of marital harmony. Or any other kind of harmony.

Then again, nothing could really prepare you for finding out your spouse was cheating on you with a colleague. He tipped his glass again and said the only thing he could think of. "At least they're moving out of state."

Evidently Theresa was letting no grass grow under her feet. Snow's ex was busy scheduling another wedding.

"Let's agree neither of us is getting involved with women ever again."

Kaleb laughed. "Define *involved*." He'd pretty much gotten his relationship skills honed to a very rigid set of requirements. No women who had a significant other. No lasting ties. No sleeping over. Actually he didn't have women over at his house anymore period. He went to their place or found other more inventive ways of getting physically close.

"That's easy. No rings. No strings. No walking the aisle. No sleeping—"

Kaleb held up a hand. "We're not allowed to sleep?"

"Funny. You know what I mean."

Unfortunately he did. Relationships were hard. He had no idea how his mom and dad had navigated thirty-five years of marital bliss, but they had. And they were still very much in love. So was his sister, who was expecting her second child. But as much as Kaleb might wish otherwise, he was not like them. His relationship track record was a royal failure with two broken engagements. He was not looking to add a third to that list.

"You were the one who actually got married, Snow, not me."

"Way to rub it in, pal. But whatever you do, don't find out the hard way what marriage is really about, like I did."

Kaleb already had, and it hadn't taken marriage to do that. Just two different women. One who'd insisted they have a baby right away, when he was just starting medical school. He'd said no, even though he wanted a family. Eventually. When things settled down. But no matter how much he tried to explain that fact, she'd kept pushing. When an ovulation tracking chart had fallen out of her purse, he knew the relationship was doomed. And maybe even his shot at fatherhood, since he was now swearing off women.

His second engagement was just as much of a flop. Candice thought a doctor that specialized in facial reconstruction meant having a plastic surgeon at her beck and call. After all, she'd landed a few parts on Broadway and had her sights set on Hollywood. Unfortunately for her, Kaleb had chosen his profession to help people with disfiguring injuries or conditions. She'd found that out when he'd gone on his first medical mission.

Why go there when you could make more money staying home?

That particular relationship had ended on an even uglier note than his first one. He'd broken off the engagement before he left on his trip and had thankfully come home to an empty apartment. Candice had cleaned out her stuff and most of his furniture, as well. It was a small price to pay to get her out of his life. So Snow wasn't the only one who'd learned the hard way.

"I have no intention of ever getting married. Two engagements were enough for me."

"Best decision you'll ever make." He raised a hand to get a second drink. "You want another?"

Kaleb had only taken a sip of his so far. "No. And I think you're going to need a designated driver, at this rate."

"You sure? We could always call a cab. After all, it's a celebration."

Except Snow's face had a hardness to it that belied his words.

"Let's not call it a celebration. How about calling it a resolution." When the bartender set a new drink in front of his friend, Kaleb lifted his glass. "To confirmed bachelorhood."

Snow raised his own. "To being smarter."

"I'll drink to that." And while Kaleb merely tasted his whiskey, his friend drained his second glass.

He had a feeling it was going to be a very long night. And he might just have to revise his no-sleeping-over policy, because his friend was probably going to be sacking out on his new sofa.

But Snow was right about one thing—Kaleb was going to learn from his friend's mistake. And his own. No more asking someone to move in with him. No more engagement rings. No kids. That one made him take a hard swallow.

And the biggest taboo of all? Walking down a very long aisle. One lined with dying flowers and broken promises, and where the only exit was a very expensive piece of paper—just like the one Snow had just signed.

No, it wasn't worth it.

To bachelorhood. The two words rolled silently through his head. If he got nothing else out of tonight, he was going to carry that thought with him and make it his own personal creed.

CHAPTER ONE

Six months later

KALEB WOKE UP to an empty bed. And sunlight streaming through the window of the swanky hotel.

Where was he? And why was he…?

He sat up in a hurry. Whoa. He'd spent the entire night there? Holy hell.

For him, that was unheard of. It was one of his taboos, along with several other things. The only explanation that made any sense was he'd been more exhausted than he thought last night. After the awful day he'd had, it was no wonder.

Snatches of the previous evening came back to haunt him: the soft, insistent press of kisses on his body. Hands that skimmed pleasure points he didn't even know he had. And an explosion that had taken him down a rabbit hole, where the experience was repeated several times. His body reacted to the memories.

But to spend the night?

Damn. Thank God she hadn't waited around for him to wake up. That might have been awkward, no matter how spectacularly she'd fit against him. No matter how intoxicating her fragrance was. No, he would have just kissed her on the lips and said his goodbyes. He paused. Well, the goodbyes might have come after he'd acted out a few more scenes with…

Nicola.

He murmured the name in his head. Tasted it on his tongue. He didn't know her last name. It hadn't been important at the time. All that had mattered was the way her eyes had touched on him in the bar and then returned several times. There'd been a hint of uncertainty in their depths that had done a number on him. So he'd gone over and bought her a drink. One that she'd accepted. A half hour later, they were out of there and in a hotel room. And what happened next had been…

Heaven.

No. Not heaven. Just another night. Just another woman.

Except he'd slept there—his arm holding her naked form to his—instead of getting up and gathering his clothes, like he normally did. Why? Was it the thrill of being there with a perfect stranger?

Maybe, except he'd had one-night stands before this. And that he was dissecting his reasons for staying made him think that something had been different this time.

Only it wasn't. Maybe it was a good thing he hadn't asked what her full name was.

Avoiding commitment was the best decision he'd ever made. Whatever his reasons for staying over, they didn't change that fact.

He lay back, lacing his fingers together behind his head. He would probably never see this Nicola person again, unless she frequented that bar, and he was pretty sure that was the first time he'd ever seen her there. She'd been alone. No wing person, not that she'd needed one. And that trace of something in her gaze had awoken instincts he'd thought were long dead.

Maybe not dead. But they'd been submerged in a sea of disillusionment.

Hell. He did not want to start tracing the origins of that word.

He pried himself out of bed and strode to the shower, turning it on full blast. He had about an hour before he needed to be at work, so he would change once he got to his office. Soon he would be able to put all thoughts of last night and the mystery woman out of his head, and get back to life as he knew it. Life as he wanted to know it. Without any Candices or Melanies or Nicolas cluttering it up and making him wonder if he'd made the wrong decision about remaining a bachelor. About not being a father. He hadn't. It had been the best thing he'd ever done. And nothing, or no *one*, was going to convince him otherwise.

Nicola's mind was wandering, and her thoughts slid in and out of places that were best left for another time. The hospital was huge and the names of people she'd been introduced to were starting to squish together inside the confines of her skull.

And as the space grew even tighter, something had to give. So squeezing between the cracks came the memory of a night five weeks ago. And the tall stranger she'd fallen into bed with.

She swallowed. She still couldn't believe she'd done that. What had she been thinking?

She hadn't been. And that had been the idea. She hadn't wanted to think, to talk… to remember. She'd just wanted to feel. And, God, had she ever. She'd…

"Kaleb, could you come over here for a moment?" Harvey Smith's voice shocked her back to reality, making her blink. "I want you to meet the newest member of our team, Nicola Bradley. Her specialty is internal medicine with an emphasis on diagnostics. She'll be helping us crack the tough cases."

As the hospital administrator continued to speak, she turned to greet the newcomer, and a wave of shock knocked her flat, setting off all kinds of sirens and alarms.

"Nicola, meet Kaleb Sabat. He's New York City Memorial's chief of reconstructive surgery."

She somehow met the man's cool blue eyes without flinching. How was this even possible? Was this some sort of cosmic joke? If so, the punch line was lost on her.

The man she'd shared a crazy, impulsive

night of sex with was NYC Memorial's chief of reconstructive surgery? Oh, God. What should she do? What *could* she do?

Quit? Run down the hallway until she found the nearest exit? No. Nicola was no chicken. At least she hoped not.

She was going to pretend it never happened, that's what she'd do. And hope that he did the same. Or maybe he didn't even remember her.

Please, God...

"Nice to meet you, Dr. Sabat," she murmured, placing the slightest emphasis on his title.

The man's head tilted sideways for a second, his eyebrows coming together as a host of changes came over his face, the last of which was sardonic amusement.

Oh, no. He remembered. *Remembered!*

They'd both had a little too much to drink that night five weeks ago, and she'd hoped...

If she'd had any idea he'd worked at the hospital she was transferring to, she would have moved off that barstool quicker than anyone believed possible. But she'd been grieving and needed to forget.

Kaleb had given her a few hours of respite…and more.

But it was behind her. Needed to stay behind her.

"You live here in the city?" His sharp eyes were on her. Watching.

She blinked. "I do now. I just moved from a facility in New Jersey." She shifted, hoping he wouldn't see something in her expression that gave her away.

"Oh? Which facility?"

Aware that the hospital administrator was taking in their conversation, she flipped her hair over her shoulder, then regretted the move when Kaleb's eyes followed the gesture. "Grace Central. It's a small private clinic."

"I'm familiar with it. It specializes in research and grants, does it not?"

That surprised her. Most people had no idea Grace Central even existed. But it had been where she'd landed after finishing up medical school. A few years later, she'd branched out, into consulting on cases from neighboring clinics, before her hospital's administrator—a man who'd been like a second father to her—pulled her aside and said that while he knew Nicola loved working there, she could do more good at one of the bigger hospitals, as much as he hated to lose her. But after her brother, who'd also worked there had... Well, she'd needed to leave. Find someplace new. Someplace that didn't have those devastating memories attached to it.

"It does. Why?" She clamped her jaws shut as she felt herself grow defensive. One of her worst personality traits, but it was really none of his business why she'd decided to move to NYC Memorial.

"No reason."

She was very glad he didn't refer to the night they'd spent together or tell Harvey that they'd already met. Repeatedly. In more ways than one.

"Actually a good friend suggested I transfer here, and I agreed with his assessment. It's a wonderful opportunity. One I couldn't pass up."

Something else chased across Kaleb's face—speculation. "Yes, it would be a shame to let opportunities like this pass you by, wouldn't it."

Before she could work through his meaning, Harvey spoke, drawing her attention back to where it should be. "Yes, indeed. I think you'll like working here. Thousands of patients come through our doors every month. We pride ourselves on trying to give each of them the answers they need. Kaleb had a tough case himself last month. I told him to take some time off, but he wouldn't hear of it. That's the kind of dedication we like to see."

Last month. Was that tough case part of the reason he'd wound up in that bar slugging back whiskey like it was water?

"Positive outcome, I hope."

"I'm afraid not."

Her glance jerked back to Kaleb's face. Not a muscle moved in those hard features, but those piercing eyes had chilled even further.

"I'm so sorry." It was hard to imagine what kind of case a plastic surgeon would find difficult other than some kind of body dysmorphic disorder, but as neither of them offered more details there was no way of knowing.

Had the patient felt lost? Like there was no way out? The way her brother had?

"It's why we're so glad you're here."

Kaleb held out his hand. "Sorry. I've got to run. I have a patient in a few minutes. Nice to meet you, Dr.... Bradley." The amusement was back. It was in the way he said her last name. Maybe because she'd purposely avoided telling him her full name.

A hesitation on her part would have given her away, so she slid her hand into his and forced herself not to shudder as the contact set her nerve endings to dancing. It was a reminder of all the other places he'd made her body dance.

Then it was over, and Kaleb was striding down the hallway away from them. She drew a shaky breath, then released it.

Harvey chuckled. "Sorry. Kaleb can be a little rough around the edges at times, but he's a good doctor. One of the best we have."

She bet. He was one of the best she'd ever had, too. That was part of the problem with seeing him again. It had been a whole lot easier being uninhibited when she'd thought they'd be going their own separate ways. And now a part of her cringed at the explicit things she'd said…and done. She'd never been like that with anyone before. Not even her ex. At the time, she'd chalked it up to the liquid courage the bartender had placed in front of her. But she had a feeling it was the man himself that had drawn those things from her.

Things she didn't even know she was capable of.

The only good thing she could pull from her current situation was that it wasn't likely she would be working with Kaleb on a regular basis. It was more probable she'd be paired up with cases from neurology or oncology, or even orthopedics. But reconstruction was, for the most part, cut-and-dried. No sifting among ambiguous symptoms to find a root cause of illness.

And yet, Harvey said he'd had a hard case. Had offered him time off.

She couldn't stop herself from asking. "You mentioned Dr. Sabat had had a difficult case not long ago."

"Yes. Tragic, really. A twenty-five-year-old came in with what was thought to be a deviated septum. She'd always had problems with snoring, and having what she said was clogged sinuses. A sleep study had ruled out apnea, so she and her husband met with Kaleb to discuss surgery. He sent her for imaging to see what he would be working with." The man sighed. "Everyone was shocked when there turned out to be a tumor in her nasal cavity. A biopsy showed primary melanoma, which had spread to her brain. As you know, it's a rare place for melanoma to start. Unfortunately, the patient went home after hearing the diagnosis and ended her life."

A horrified shudder went through her. What were the chances? That had to be why he'd been at the bar that night. They'd both had something they wanted to forget. Needed to forget.

And now, all Nicola wanted to do was forget what her "wanting to forget" had caused.

"I've read about melanoma occurring in the nasal cavity, but have never been involved in a case. It carries a poor prognosis, doesn't it? And with it having already metastasized…"

"Yes. And because she'd always had sinus issues and just considered it a minor annoyance, it took longer for her to get fed up enough to seek help. By then, it was probably too late. It's tragic no matter how you look at it."

Yes, it was. "For her husband, as well."

"She also had two toddlers at home."

"God." She couldn't imagine the emotional pain the woman had gone through. And to leave two toddlers behind? Nicola was about ten years older than Kaleb's patient and had no children of her own. Although she'd always hoped someday…

"How terrible."

"It was a blow to everyone who worked on her case. Kaleb took it especially hard." He shook his head. "Well, let's finish showing you around so you can get back to your day. Are you starting next week?"

"Yes. I've wrapped up all of my cases at Grace Central, so I should be good to start on Monday."

"Perfect."

Showing her around and introducing her to some of the other staff members took another hour. If names and titles had blurred together before, they now had stopped registering at all. Especially after the shock of seeing Kaleb again.

The administrator opened the door to yet another room. "And this will be your office."

"My…?" She blinked. She actually hadn't expected to have four walls and a door to call her own. Grace Central had an open office concept, so there were very few private offices outside of two conference rooms. Most of the staff worked in areas that were divided into sections that, while a step up from cubicles, would definitely not qualify as offices. They were more like wide melamine shelves with a chair underneath. Just to house a computer and maybe a picture or two.

"I really don't think I need something this…big." What Nicola meant was that she didn't really need anything with a door.

Harvey glanced inside and then at her with a smile. "This is one of our smaller offices, actually. I was afraid you might feel insulted."

"Not insulted at all."

He was right. The space wasn't large. It housed a desk with two office chairs in front of it and a bookcase behind. There was a coatrack to the side and a laptop already on top of the desk. As if reading the question on her face, he nodded. "We'd rather you use our computer equipment rather than your personal laptop due to privacy concerns."

She could understand that. "This seems like a luxury compared to what I had before."

He glanced around again, maybe trying to understand her reservations. "You'll be meeting with doctors and patients alike, so it's better to have a place to do that rather than having to keep checking to see if there's a room open on the fourth floor. It's where all of our conference rooms are."

This hospital had one whole floor dedicated to meeting space? It was going to take some getting used to. Grace Central's staff was close-knit and worked well together, probably because of the small size. But after her brother's death, the words of consolation had become too unbearable. She had several friends there that she'd promised to keep in touch with. She had a feeling it would be a lot harder to forge those kinds of relationships in a hospital as large as NYC Memorial, where she knew no one.

Strike that. She knew one person.

Really? "Knew" might be stretching it a little. Although learning about his patient had been a jolt. And it was good to know he didn't normally hang out drinking his troubles away at a bar.

Yikes. Is that what he thought she did? Maybe she should set him straight at some point. The last thing she wanted was for him to think NYC Memorial's newest doctor had a drinking problem. Or go to Harvey with his "concerns" and ignite all kinds of questions and rumors.

Yes. She was going to have a little chat with Dr. Sabat and set some things straight.

Except she'd pretended not to know him. So that might be a very awkward conversation. She wavered a second or two before deciding to let it drop. If he told on her, she could just as easily tell on him.

And now she was acting like they were both children, ready to retaliate against each other. They weren't. At least she wasn't. Unless his behavior endangered his patients, she wasn't about to say anything to anyone about what had happened. And she definitely wouldn't mention it to Kaleb.

So she was going to put that night into her past. Once and for all.

She decided to speak what she hoped would become a prophetic statement. "I love the office and the hospital. I have a feeling I'm going to be very happy at NYC Memorial."

CHAPTER TWO

NICOLA WAITED FOR the explosion. The one that normally accompanied challenging a surgeon's diagnosis.

Dr. Danvers held up his hand when the intern standing next to him looked like he was going to argue Danvers's point. "So you're saying what we saw on the MRI slides is an incidental finding. Care to explain your reasoning?"

How was she going to convince him that the conclusion from two doctors—that the patient's condition was due to a brain tumor—was really something else entirely? Something a whole lot more simple. Something that wouldn't involve cutting open the patient's skull and digging around with a scalpel. It would be easier to let them go in and send off a sample to pathology and have her idea confirmed, but why do that when she could show them another possibility?

Out of the corner of her eye, she saw someone push through the door to the staff lounge.

Great. Kaleb. Just the person she was trying to avoid.

He made his way over to them, and, of course, Dr. Danvers had to fill him in on what they were talking about.

Eying her, Kaleb said, "What do you think it is?"

"A bit of fat."

Dr. Danvers stared at her as if in disbelief. "Fat."

"You *know* it happens. You see something on the film that you don't like. Something that looks nefarious and assume that it's the worst-case scenario. We all do it."

"Sometimes it *is* the worst-case scenario." Kaleb folded his arms across his chest.

Was he thinking of his own patient? The one who'd had malignant melanoma? Hadn't her own brother's misdiagnoses over the years turned out to be far worse than anyone believed possible?

Something inside of her turned soft as compassion swirled to life. "Yes. Sometimes it is.

But not always. Let's do another scan. With contrast, this time. Surely waiting another day or two won't make a difference at this point. And if, God forbid, it is a tumor, there's no sign of it having spread. But if we take another look, using a different technique, we might be able to know for sure. She's young. Her brain is still developing."

Kaleb glanced at Danvers. "She's got a point."

That surprised her. Especially since his last statement had carried a pessimism that made her chest tighten.

She knew that feeling all too well. But she couldn't let it cloud her judgment about other cases. If she did, the temptation to over test, over treat, would always be there whispering in her ear. Instead, she was somehow able to push her brother's case into a little compartment, one she kept locked tight. Except for that one time—when she'd gone to a bar and let it consume her, hoping by drowning it, she could finally come to terms with it. Only she'd done much more than drink that night. She'd let a moment of impulse direct her to a hotel room. A lapse in judgment that she was having a very hard time kicking aside.

Especially seeing that lapse standing here in the flesh.

Dr. Danvers and the intern glanced at each other and Danvers finally shrugged. "Okay. Let's order up another study—with contrast this time—and see what we get. But, I want to be very clear here…if the new scan doesn't look any different, we'll be recommending surgery to her parents."

That was fair. All she'd wanted was a hearing. For them to take a breath before jumping into something that couldn't be taken back.

Like she'd done with Kaleb? Jumping into something that couldn't be taken back?

"If that happens, I'll back you up a hundred percent. But I really feel it's not a malignancy."

"We'll see." Dr. Danvers and his partner in crime retreated, but not before throwing a pointed look at Kaleb that she couldn't quite read.

Once they were gone, Kaleb nodded at a nearby table in the cafeteria. "Still taking advantage of every opportunity that comes your way?"

"Excuse me?"

He shook his head. "Never mind. Do you have a minute?"

She tensed. Was he going to bring up the night at the bar or what had happened after they wound up in a hotel room? Oh, Lord, she hoped not. Especially since she'd been thinking about just that when the NYC Memorial's administrator had been introducing her to people. Then to realize that Kaleb was actually here, at her new hospital… "Sure."

She dropped into one of the lounge's seats before her legs decided to desert her. She'd been pretty successful at steering clear of him, not that it was hard in a hospital this size.

"Coffee?"

"Yes, please. One sugar, no cream." It would give her a minute or two to compose herself after her confrontation with Danvers and his intern. There hadn't been an explosion, but she could tell both doctors had been irritated with her. But they'd come to her with the question, not the other way around. It wasn't like she was some ambulance chaser trying to drum up business. If her time at Grace Central was any indication of how things would go in New York, she wouldn't have to chase anyone. She would have more work than she'd have time for very soon.

He came back with the coffee and set hers in front of her. "So how are things going so far?"

Instead of her tension draining away at the question, it coiled in her gut, squeezing tight. There seemed to be some secondary meaning behind almost everything he said to her. It had to be her imagination. Right? "Things are going fine. It's all pretty new, though."

She'd moved into her office exactly a week ago. But in that short period of time, she'd had a couple of run-ins like she'd had with Danvers. She considered it part of her job to question things, to be that little devil sitting on someone's shoulder.

"Danvers is a pretty nice guy, you'll find. Quite reasonable, actually."

Was he saying she wasn't? "Really? Why would that matter to me?"

He stared at her for a minute or two. "They're going to be your colleagues, Nicola. Hell, they already are."

The squeezing inside tightened even more. "Ah. I get it. Don't challenge the good-old-boy way of doing things."

"That's not what I'm saying at all." He sighed. "Look, I wish you'd been here when that case I'd had landed on my desk. I'm sure Harvey filled you in on what happened."

"He did, and I'm sorry." Her brother's face swirled in front of her, dredging up the sick feeling of horror she'd had. She forced the emotion back to the pit of her stomach.

"It's why I went…" He shook his head. "Never mind. None of that matters."

She took a sip of coffee. He wasn't the enemy. He was trying to help. "Sorry. My answer just now was defensive. So was the way I approached Dr. Danvers. It's just that it's sometimes hard to get a hearing, especially if I'm not patting someone on the back and telling them exactly what they want to hear. There are times when, instead of letting them go ahead and do the treatment their way, I have to disagree and speak my mind. It's why I was hired. And, believe me, it's not always easy for me. In fact, it's damn hard, so I know I sometimes come across as a—"

"Hard ass?"

She laughed. "Wow, you don't pull any punches, do you?"

"No more than you do."

"Touché. But in the end, my concern has to be for the well-being of the patient, rather than worrying about soothing another doctor's ego."

"Which is, like you said, exactly why Harvey brought you in. But that also means there might be some feelings of resentment, in the sense that some might feel the hospital's administrator is overstepping his bounds—as if he's looking over their shoulders and busting their chops."

She hadn't really thought about it that way. Her opinions had been respected, for the most part, at Grace Central. So to find out there was some animosity toward her at her current hospital was a hard pill to swallow. "What do you suggest I do?"

"Collaborate."

She frowned. "I thought that's what I was doing."

"Is it?"

Looking back at her interaction with the two doctors a few minutes ago, she could acknowledge the brusqueness in her responses. "I guess it's hard to be challenged."

"It is. And that works both ways. People

tend to mimic the tone they sense in someone else."

"And my tone wasn't pleasing to the ear?"
This time the words were accompanied by a
smile to show she was joking.

He laughed. "Like you said. It's hard to be
challenged. And for the record, I hope you're
right about the patient."

"Me, too. Especially after what you just
said."

"Looking forward to delivering the I-told-
you-so?"

"No. Hoping that a little girl doesn't need
brain surgery."

He rested his forearms on the table and
stared at her. "If you're right and the MRI
image was just a piece of fat, what is causing
her diplopia? Or did you already share that
with Dr. Danvers?"

"I haven't seen all of the tests yet. Just the
MRI reading. But I plan to review the case
tonight when I get home."

"Why not do it right now? I'd like to see
your process."

"Here in the cafeteria?"

"How about in my office?"

She wasn't sure how she felt about having someone watch her. It reminded her of his comment about the hospital administrator looking over someone's shoulder. "My process isn't all that exciting. It basically consists of me staring at a piece of paper for a long time and then muttering to myself. Repeatedly."

"That's okay. I've been known to mutter from time to time myself."

Sudden heat washed up her neck and into her face. She'd been a witness to that muttering. Only what she remembered most were the things he'd said with his lips pressed tight to her throat. Not to mention his…

Oh, Lord. This was the last thing she should be thinking about. Especially since she didn't want him to know she remembered that night. It was a whole lot easier to just sit here and pretend they only knew each other from work.

Because it was the truth. She knew about his lovemaking—and that was some pretty fantastic stuff—but she didn't know him as a person.

She still didn't. And if she were smart she would make sure it stayed that way. Which meant having him watch her work would be excruciating. But if she turned him down, he would wonder why and maybe start asking questions she really didn't want to answer. Like maybe about a certain night. Or her reasons for being in that bar.

So she'd let him watch. And satisfy his curiosity, she hoped.

Then after they were done, she would steer clear of both Dr. Sabat and her memories of that night in the hotel room.

He'd hoped he was wrong. That he'd imagined she didn't remember him. But evidently she really didn't. Once the shock of seeing her had worn off, he'd watched her face for some hint that she was simply trying to hide from Harvey the fact that they'd had a one-night stand. In fact, he'd been mentally rehearsing what to say if she told the administrator they'd already met.

He hadn't needed to say anything. Her "nice to meet you" had been smooth and polite. And totally believable. Even to him. She had him doubting his memories of that night. Until she bit the corner of her lip, the way she had that night. Whenever he'd done something she liked.

Like lick the little hollow at the base of her throat. Or touch…

Don't go there, Kaleb.

But as that firm bottom swished back and forth in front of him with each step she took, it was damn hard not to relive those memories. It was also damn hard to understand why this was so difficult. He'd always been able to keep his professional life separate from his personal one. He'd done it ever since his breakup with his ex.

But then again, he'd never had a woman forget she'd slept with him before.

That had to be the difference. His ego was wounded.

One side of his mouth went up. Isn't that what she'd said? That she wasn't interested in stroking anyone's ego? Well, maybe not, but she'd seemed pretty interested in stroking his…

Hell! Knock it off, dammit!

They got to her office, and she unlocked the door and went in, and he finally managed to remove his gaze from her ass and focus on the interior of the room.

It was as stark and unadorned as her words to Dr. Danvers had been. "I like what you've done to the place. Looks like you're making yourself at home." He couldn't hide the slight irony behind the words.

She swung around to look at him and then glanced at the space. "I wasn't actually expecting to have an office, so I decided to wait and make sure this wasn't some kind of mistake."

It took him a second to realize she was joking. Well, maybe not the part about having an office, but the rest. "I'm pretty sure you're supposed to at least put a family photo on your desk, so your patients know you're not a robot."

Her face changed in a millisecond, a stricken look coming over it. There was a huge pause. "I'm not a robot."

This time she wasn't joking. Maybe his earlier words had stung more than he'd meant them to. "I'm sorry. I never meant to imply you were."

"I know. You were kidding. So was I."

No, she hadn't been. And there was still a strained look at the corners of her eyes. Like he'd said something that had struck a nerve. But he was at a loss to figure out what.

Her lips twisted. "Putting a family picture

in here might be a little problematic for me. And my family."

"Oh?"

"My brother passed away recently, so I'm not quite ready to stare at a picture of him every time I come into this room. To see him smiling and full of life would be hard right now."

Shock froze his vocal cords for a second before he recovered. "Hell, Nicola, I didn't know. I'm really sorry."

"It's okay." She pulled in a deep breath, then let it out on an audible note. "It was so... unexpected, and we're all still grieving. So yes. Complicated to put a picture in here. Do I display one with him in it? Omit him, as if he'd never existed? And if my parents come to visit me at the hospital, it might make things harder on them."

"I can see how that might." He wanted to ask what had happened, but it was none of his business, and like she'd just said, it might make it harder on her. His earlier thoughts about the way her bottom swished seemed way out of line in light of what she'd just revealed.

"Anyway, that's not why you came to my

office, right? To admire the decor? Or lack of it?"

No. The only decor he'd admired so far had been her. But that was going to stop right here, right now. It was how he'd ended up in two very bad relationships. It also made him decide not to ask about that evening. Especially since he'd been so shocked to find he'd spent the entire night there. If she wasn't going to bring it up, then neither was he. After all, what good would it do? And she didn't seem worried about him saying anything to anyone, so she probably really didn't remember. Or had her reasons for keeping quiet about it.

"Nope. So how do you want to do this? With me behind your desk? Or you in front of it?"

Her eyes widened. "Pardon me?"

Damn. He was losing it. It had to be the shock of what she'd said. "To look at the scans on your computer."

Her shoulders seemed to relax in a rush. "Got it. Sorry. I don't know what I was thinking."

Well, that made two of them, because he

didn't know what the hell he was thinking, either.

"Let's sit in front of it. It'll be easier." She swiveled her screen around and moved her keyboard in front of one of the two chairs, then grabbed a large spiral-bound notebook off her desk.

Well, the paper and pen seemed a little low-tech, but then again, he liked to write his thoughts by hand and then enter them into the computer later, too. "It seems we agree on one thing, anyway," he said.

"What's that?" She came around and sank into her chair, waiting for him to do the same.

"You take handwritten notes."

She flipped her notebook open to a bookmarked page and set it on the desk, then turned it toward him. "I tend to think in linear terms, and since I don't have a whiteboard in my office yet, this is how I'm doing it."

It was actually more of a sketchbook than a notebook, and he saw why. On the sheet in front of him was something that looked like a series of filled-in rectangles with lines going here, there and everywhere.

"This was a case I had at Grace Central." She pointed at the top row. "I write down symptoms in the order they happen and draw a line toward possible causes. I keep going until the lines begin to converge."

Her pen moved to the third row, where some of the conditions had only one line drawn to them, while others had multiples. "Then I move the most likely down a row and start all over again, asking the patient questions about other things they may or may not have noticed. Sometimes, after living with some kind of minor irritation for a period of time, it becomes a type of background noise that gets drowned out by the more pressing symptoms."

He noticed that she'd added hair loss to the new row. He tapped a finger on it. "So this was one of those minor issues she hadn't noticed?"

"Yes. She started noticing more hair tangled in her hairbrush, along with gradual weight gain, which she attributed to menopausal symptoms."

"But it wasn't."

"I didn't think so. So we worked our way down to a group of subsets and ran a more narrow spectrum of tests to see what, if anything, it added to our search."

The test results were added to the graph, and this time the lines all converged on one diagnosis: Hashimoto's, an autoimmune condition where the body's cells attack healthy tissue. In this case, the thyroid.

"Amazing. Okay, so I take back the part about our processes being similar. This goes way beyond anything I do."

"I bet you do other things that are equally amazing," she said, before her face flamed to life, and she suddenly became very interested in switching between her computer screens.

If he didn't know better, he'd think there was something more behind those words. As if she might actually remember...

No. It was probably just like when he'd said something that could be construed a different way. Except she hadn't tried to correct herself and say she was talking about his work.

Good try, Kaleb. It really does bother you that she doesn't remember that crazy sex you had together.

And it had been crazy. The brusque attitude she now carried around with her at work had been nowhere to be seen. Instead she'd been...

Incredibly sexy. Scorchingly hot.

Unforgettable.

And that last word was the one that bothered him the most. Because he couldn't seem to shake it off, no matter how hard he tried. Was it just the juxtaposition between the raw sensuality of that night and the chilly aloofness she'd shown him at work? It made for a combination that intrigued him. Made him want to explore that contrast a little more in depth.

But he wasn't going to. And from her attitude, she would not welcome him asking her out on a date.

And then there was the issue of keeping his personal life separate from his private life. It had been working just fine for him so far. And Snow would laugh him out of town if he knew how he was dwelling on this, especially after that toast they'd made last winter.

Nicola's voice pulled him back from his thoughts.

"So here's what we know about Dr. Danvers's patient so far. She developed diplopia in her left eye about four months ago. Right eye is normal. A trip to an optometrist, followed by an appointment with an ophthalmologist, revealed no structural problems with the eye other than some astigmatism. Before this incident, her vision had been twenty-twenty. It's still perfect in her right eye, but her left eye has double vision. Enough to interfere with her daily activities."

He nodded. "I can see why Danvers ordered an MRI. And why he assumed the shadow was a microadenoma, especially since it's near her pituitary gland. A growing tumor can cause vision problems."

"Yes. The only thing that bothers me is that a microadenoma of that size shouldn't cause as much disruption in her vision as the patient has. Now a macroadenoma, that's a different story."

Strangely, Kaleb was enjoying listening to her bouncing around ideas. It was no different than the back-and-forth he'd shared with other colleagues, wasn't it? Except he hadn't slept with his other colleagues.

"So what else besides a tumor could be causing the problem?" He nodded at the screen. "We have her vision tests from two years ago that show her with perfect vision."

"Lots of things. Multiple sclerosis. Myasthenia gravis. Stroke. Guillain-Barré—"

"Yes, I've seen something as simple as

heavy eyelids causing vision changes as people age. But this patient is young."

"Yes, she is." She tapped her pencil on the paper of her sketchbook and then started writing up a chart much like the one she'd just shown him. "I hadn't thought about eyelid weight. Or something else affecting the eyelids. Any mention of chalazions?"

He wasn't sure if the question was directed toward him, but she was suddenly moving through different doctors' reports and tests. "Hmm…not seeing it."

"What does that mean?"

"It means I would like to meet with her and ask a couple of questions. Do you think Danvers would object to me talking to his patient?"

"I can't see why not. Like I said earlier, he's a pretty reasonable guy."

She smiled. "Yes, you did. Right before you told me I wasn't."

"I never said you weren't reasonable."

"Not in so many words. But I'm pretty good at reading between the lines."

He held up a hand. "There was nothing there to read, I swear. I only said that you and Danvers were now colleagues and that you might want to take a more measured approach."

"In other words, be more reasonable?" Her eyebrows went up and she turned to meet his gaze.

"Looks like I'm not going to win this particular argument."

"Do you want to? Win, I mean?"

He leaned back and crossed his arms over his chest. "Not particularly. Especially not this kind of argument. If I'm in it to win, it needs to have a pretty big payoff at the end."

"I totally agree. When that happens, I have a fight-to-win, take-no-prisoners mentality."

He clapped a hand to his chest. "Should I be worried?"

"Not today…" She gave a soft laugh that was very attractive.

He glanced at her face and liked what he saw. It's what had drawn him to her in the bar. That delicate bone structure and the hint of crow's feet at the corners of her eyes. It was an indication that she liked to smile. And although he hadn't seen as much of that particular feature here at work, the evidence was there for all to see.

And she'd smiled a lot that night as she'd sipped her drink.

Then again, so had he. Only his smile had been fake. He'd been shocked by the events surrounding a patient and had needed a drink. Or two or three. By the end of that night, neither he nor Nicola had been under the legal limit, so they'd shared a cab. And instead of having it take them home, they'd made out in the back seat, and then asked the driver to drop them off at a hotel. The rest was history.

Well, his history, since Nicola didn't seem to remember that night.

Her brother had died. She'd said it had been recent. As in before their night together? Or after it?

On impulse, he leaned closer and covered her hand with his. He realized it was a mistake when the softness of her skin reminded him of how much he'd enjoyed stroking it. Kissing it. He cleared his throat so he could force out the words. "Hey, I really am sorry about your brother."

Her eyes met his for a long moment, then she said, "Thanks. I appreciate it. It's been hard. On me. On my parents. He worked with me at Grace Central as a researcher. If we could have known what was coming… Well, maybe things might have been different."

"How so?"

"I don't know. We could have talked to him. Tried to make sure he knew that we would always be there for him. That we wanted him there with us."

A chill went up his spine, a type of déjà vu that never boded well for what was about to follow.

"Had he been sick?"

Her hand shifted under his, index finger hooking over his as if needing to hold on to something. He had a feeling she wasn't even aware of what she'd done. But it was doing a number on his gut—a strange protective instinct rose up, just like it had at the bar.

"He'd been diagnosed with ankylosing spondylitis."

"Damn." Ankylosing spondylitis was a devastating inflammatory condition where bones of the back, or even ribs, could fuse, causing pain and severe loss of motion, sometimes to the point of impeding respiration. "That doesn't normally carry a death sentence, though."

"Not directly, no, but for a man who prided

himself on being strong and fit—he loved to windsurf, sail and go mountain climbing—it was a life-altering diagnosis. To him, it might as well have been a death sentence. And it ultimately became one."

"Did he have complications from treatment?"

She gave a visible swallow. "No, Kaleb, he didn't. Danny died before he ever started treatment. He received his diagnosis, then went home and ended his life. My dad found him the next day when I called saying Danny hadn't arrived at work yet. I asked Dad to check on him. Something I wished I'd never done, because..." She shook her head. "Well, it's why having his picture on my desk right now would be so hard."

His throat squeezed at the pain in her voice and a million thoughts and emotions went through him. It was so eerily similar to what had happened with his melanoma patient. The despair and fear that both of them must have felt. Damn. They'd been caught between a rock and a hard place with what seemed like no way out.

"Damn, Nicola. I had no idea."

She let out a laugh that was far from amused

and took her hand from his, using it to flip through the pages of her sketchbook. Back, back, back she went, stopping at a page and staring at it. "He told me he'd been having some hip and back pain, and so I did up one of my nifty little charts. When I asked if he was having light sensitivity—never dreaming he'd answer yes—my world shifted. Became a dark hole. I wanted to scrub away everything I'd written down and pretend like I didn't know. Except I did."

Nicola pointed to a box that had the condition listed. The word *no!* appeared as a long silent scream on the page. She'd known it was going to be a devastating blow to her brother, especially with what she'd said about his lifestyle.

"Did you break the news to him?"

"No. I—I couldn't. I referred him to a doctor friend, telling that friend what I suspected. The sooner treatment is started, to knock down the inflammation, the better. Tests were rushed and for once, I prayed I was wrong. I would have given *anything* to be wrong, Kaleb."

"I know."

One shoulder went up in a half shrug, and

her chin wobbled. "But I wasn't." Her voice lowered to a whisper. "Oh, God, I wasn't. And Danny…"

He couldn't stop himself from wrapping an arm around her shoulder and drawing her close. "I can't imagine how hard it was to realize his pain wasn't due to simple muscle strain."

"You have no idea."

No, he didn't. His mom had endured a mastectomy and radiation treatments, but he hadn't been the one who'd diagnosed her, so as hard as that had been, it would have been even tougher if he'd had to do what Nicola had done.

She leaned her head against his chest, and Kaleb's hand slid under her hair to support her neck, the honeyed strands sliding over his skin like silk. Just like they had that night. The tightening in his throat shifted to somewhere lower, and he cursed himself. Told himself to move away. Now.

But his mind and his body seemed disconnected from each other at the moment.

His ears picked up a sigh, and she murmured against his chest, "Thank you. I'm sorry for blubbering all over your shirt. I'm not sure why it suddenly hit me again."

"Maybe because I pressed you for information, when I shouldn't have."

"It's not that. Every once in a while it just seems to build up inside of me, looking for an exit. I think that's why I ended up…"

Her words trailed away for a second, and he wondered if she was going to say it was why she'd ended up in the bar that night.

But when her voice came back, she simply said, "I think that's why I seem short sometimes when I talk to people."

It made sense. It also made him feel pretty damn crappy for lecturing her about the way she'd talked to Danvers. A good reason not to assign motive to things he knew nothing about. And she wasn't being short now. In fact, she was being…soft, approachable. And he liked it. Way too much.

And if he didn't move away, he might do something he'd regret even more than their night together.

He shifted sideways a bit, so it wouldn't seem as awkward, then moved his hand down to her shoulder and gave her what he hoped was a reassuring pat or two. She moved back upright quickly. So quickly that it knocked his hand away.

"Sorry, again." She brushed her hair off her forehead, and the movement was probably meant to cover the fact that she'd swiped the area below her eyes. "And I probably need to get ready for my next consultation, which is in less than an hour."

"Got it. I probably need to get going, as well." He pried himself from his chair and stood to his feet. "Let me know when Danvers's patient has her new MRI. I'd like to know where all your little arrows wind up."

"I will." She stood, too.

He moved toward the door, only to have her voice stop him when he gripped the handle to open it.

"Oh, and Kaleb..."

"Yes?" He glanced back at her.

"From now on, I'll try to be a little more 'colleaguey' toward those I work with. Feel free to call me out if I don't succeed."

No way was he going to do that. Especially given how he'd felt when she told him about her brother. But rather than argue, he simply nodded and pushed through the door.

As he walked down the hall, he gave himself a stiff lecture, which he quickly counter-acted. *Nothing happened, so just settle down.*

Some good advice, if he'd ever heard it.

The problem was, he'd wanted something to happen. And if he allowed it to, it might be a bigger disaster than that night in the hotel. And she might end up as a third notch on his belt of failed relationships.

CHAPTER THREE

WHY ON EARTH had she told him all of Danny's story yesterday? Maybe it was Kaleb's suggestion of putting a family picture in her office and the fact that she thought of her brother every single day. Agonized over it whenever her head hit the pillow. And Kaleb's hand had felt so damn good on hers in her office. As if he cared. Really cared.

In that moment she'd realized how much she'd needed someone besides Grace Central and her family to know what had happened to him. Someone who understood the devastating loss that suicide brought. Kaleb had lost a patient to it. And she'd lost a brother.

But once she'd said the actual words, a spurt of panic had shot through her, along with a few other emotions she hadn't wanted to dissect. The panic had been chased by a vague sense of nausea over letting someone she barely knew see her like this. But when his arm had gone around her, she'd slid right against his chest with a sense of belonging that had shocked her. Scared her. And when his warm palm had settled on the back of her neck, she'd almost melted. It was sensual and comforting and familiar, all at the same time. It was the same sensation she'd had in the bar all those weeks ago. She'd wanted to look up at him. Had wanted him to kiss her. Make her forget all over again.

Which would have been stupid. Because it hadn't changed anything that night, and it wouldn't change anything if she let it happen again. Thank God she'd snuck out of his room in the early hours of the morning, before he woke up. Better she'd left than him. It was becoming a ritual with her now. To leave before being left. She wanted to be the first one to exit a room. Or be the first one to leave a get-together. That's what losing a fiancé, followed by losing a brother, did. The thought of being left behind had evidently become a crippling force that she couldn't shake.

Because when Kaleb had been the first one to move away from her when they were in her office, she'd squirmed inside. Felt that same sense of fearful dread. Which is probably why she'd been slightly sick after the encounter. Why she'd woken up this morning with that same low-grade churning in her midsection at the thought of facing him again.

She pulled two pieces of bread out of the wrapper and slid them into her toaster, waiting for that warm smell of crisp toast to fill the air. It was weird how much she loved it. Even when she was sick, it was normally the one thing she could eat. A minute or two later, her nose twitched. Ah, right on cue. The toaster kicked the bread into the air with a sharp snap, and Nicola retrieved it, then spread some butter and a spoonful of marmalade onto each slice.

Almost as soon as she bit into the food, her stomach settled and she closed her eyes to enjoy the treat.

"See? I try to treat you right." She leaned against the counter and let the tangy blend of flavors dance across her tongue.

Dr. Danvers's diplopia patient had an appointment this afternoon for the second scan. That was a lot quicker than she'd thought it would be. But it would give her a chance to ask the patient and her parents a few more questions. If she wanted to be there on time, she'd better get a move on. After finishing her breakfast, she went to the bathroom and slapped on a little makeup, frowning at the dark circles under her eyes. Lack of sleep last night?

She shrugged and reached under the counter for the sponge to wipe out her sink, her feminine products catching her eye. Hmm, she hadn't gotten her period yet.

How long overdue was she?

Not more than a week or two. She'd never been particularly regular, so she couldn't really chart it beyond having a vague sense of when it might come. But she was wrong more often than she was right.

She always kept something in her purse just in case. Maybe that's why she'd felt a little off yesterday and this morning—she was getting ready to start. Just what she needed. But the alternative was…

She shuddered. Yeah, not what she needed on top of everything else. Besides, it wasn't like she was having a lot of sex nowadays.

Except for…

She blinked. Don't even go there. They'd

used protection and she was still within her normal parameters of a week or two late.

Besides, she couldn't do anything about it right this second. So if another week went by and nothing happened, then she'd let herself worry. But until then, she was going on with her life.

Starting with Dr. Danvers's patient.

An hour later, she sat in an exam room with Lindy MacDonald and her parents, along with Dr. Danvers. This time, his prickly intern was nowhere to be seen, for which she was glad. Lindy was being prepped for the MRI, with the neurologist explaining to the girl's parents what would happen with the contrast. They had to sign yet another consent form. Nicola noticed the mom's hand was shaking. Poor woman, she had to be scared out of her mind wondering if something was growing in her daughter's brain.

If Nicola was going to ask her questions, she'd better do it now.

"Do you mind if I ask you a couple of things?"

She'd been introduced a few minutes ago, and Danvers had given her permission to examine Lindy, as well. She was positive the surgeon had been thorough, so she skipped a physical exam. Instead she asked about any strange symptoms that she might not have attributed to her daughter's double vision, but that had occurred, nonetheless.

"No, nothing I can think of."

"What about her eyes? Besides the double vision. Any lumps or bumps or eye strain that were out of the ordinary?"

"Mom, what about that spider bite?"

"I'd forgotten about that." The woman shook her head. "But surely, that can't have anything to do with it."

"Spider bite?" Nicola leaned forward. How many times had she heard that before, that a simple symptom couldn't have anything to do with a condition, only to realize it had *everything* to do with it?

"She got this strange bump on her eyelid. I thought maybe it was a mosquito bite at first. It came and went for about six months. Every time I got ready to make a doctor's appointment, it seemed to get better. I used hot compresses and antihistamine lotion on it and eventually it faded to nothing."

"So you never took her to the doctor for

it?" She glanced at the chart to remind herself which eye they were dealing with.

"No. She said it didn't hurt or anything. Just looked like an insect bite, or maybe even a sty or something. But it was in the middle of her lid."

"Which lid?"

"Her left one."

Standing next to her, she saw Dr. Danvers stiffen. Then he moved over to the patient. Pushing his glasses onto his nose, he asked Lindy's mom, "Mind if I take a quick look?"

"No, of course not."

The surgeon tilted the girl's chin and looked closely at her. "Close your eyes, please."

Lindy shut her eyes, and Dr. Danvers used his gloved thumb to apply slight pressure to different parts of the eyelid. His gaze came up and fixed Nicola with a look. "I think there's a slight thickening here. How did you know?"

"I didn't. And I don't know for sure. Not without seeing the scans. But I've heard of cases where a large chalazion can exert enough pressure on the cornea to change its shape."

"A chalazion?" Lindy's mom came over and looked at her daughter's eyelid.

"Maybe so." Danvers looked at his patient. "I'm going to turn your lid inside out, okay?"

"Will it hurt?"

"No. It might feel a little funny, though. I want to look at the back of your lid." He quickly flipped up her lid and stared at the undersurface. "I do see a slight scarring here. Look."

Nicola came closer and saw what he did. A whitened portion in the middle of all those blood vessels.

After righting Lindy's lid, he sat on the stool across from her parents. "Your daughter may have had what's called a chalazion. It's a little different than a sty in that a sty is normally on the margin of the eyelid, whereas a chalazion's core tends to point toward the eye itself. So when it bursts, or drains, the opening will appear on the back of the lid, where it's out of sight. You may even miss it when that happens—you'll just notice that the swelling appears to subside. Just like what you described. How big would you say her swelling was?"

"Maybe the size of an M&M. Once it got even larger than that. But she said it never hurt. She was more embarrassed by what her friends might think than anything else."

Lindy said, "Because it was ugly. I'm glad it's gone."

"I am, too," Danvers said. "I still would like to do the MRI to rule out anything else, but it's possible this chalazion caused her change in vision, which would be much simpler than what we thought."

"Will it be permanent?"

"If the pressure was there for six months, it might be. The best-case scenario would be for her eye to slowly return to its former shape. It may also be why Lindy's vision has seemed to fluctuate in that eye enough to make it difficult to prescribe a corrective lens."

"We thought we were going crazy. It was like every time I took her in, they came up with a different reading. And there were times she couldn't tell which screen was clearer."

Nicola should feel a flare of pride, but that nagging sense of unease in the pit of her stomach was back, and she wasn't sure what to do about it. Could it be the case itself? That she was afraid of being wrong and being shown up? Or have someone say "I told you I was right."

No. As long as they got the right diagnosis, Nicola didn't care who came up with it.

And if it saved a patient from having brain surgery, it was worth all the discomfort in the world.

Maybe she was hungry. All she'd had for breakfast was toast. Probably not a smart move to eat nothing but carbs. Except she did that all the time with no ill effects.

"Okay, let's get her to radiology and take a closer look at that spot we saw the other day."

Lindy glanced at her. "Will you be there?"

Her face turned warm. "If you'd like me to be. I won't be able to be in the room while you're having the MRI, but I can wait right outside. Will that be okay?"

"Yes."

Nicola glanced at Dr. Danvers, who nodded and gave her a smile. A genuine one, this time. Maybe he believed her.

Why wouldn't he? It's not like she had any skin in the game. She just wanted what was best for his patient.

As did he, she reminded herself.

The contrast went smoothly, and so did the MRI. Fortunately, the patient didn't have claustrophobia, so she was in and out in forty minutes and sent back to a waiting area with her mom and dad. Danvers was going to read the scans himself, so there would be no waiting time. Kaleb was right. He was a good guy. She didn't sense any resentment, for which she was grateful. And, honestly, he would have eventually come to the same conclusion. Or at least agreed that it wasn't a tumor, even if he'd opened her up and sectioned the spot.

Sitting in his office a few minutes later, she waited tensely as he went through the scans on his computer. He pointed out several interesting things as they scrolled through, and she put the information into her mental filing cabinet for future reference.

"Okay, here we go." A slice of Lindy's pituitary gland came into view and the shadow seemed less distinct now than it had in the previous test. And nothing really stood out as abnormal.

He looked up with a sigh. "I'll have to give it to you. You were right. It's probably not a microadenoma. Just an 'incidentaloma,' like you said. Thank you for not backing down."

Kaleb's words came back to her. "Dr. Danvers, I hope you don't think I—"

"Clint, please. After all, it looks like I'll

be calling on you for consults on a regular basis."

She blinked, a sudden warmth going through her system. Was he saying he appreciated her input? He'd thanked her for not backing down, so it certainly sounded like it. She remembered his incredulous response when she'd suggested the image might show a simple piece of fatty tissue. He'd been right to be surprised. According to Kaleb, she probably hadn't helped her case by just blowing past his diagnosis and forming one of her own. Maybe she'd work on that a little. As a woman in medical school there had been times where she'd had to stand up to someone because of her gender—felt like she'd had to be a little bit bolder in order to gain a hearing, even though she'd been in the top ten of her class.

But this wasn't school, and they were all on equal footing here. So she could afford to relax a bit and enjoy the view. She'd made it. And it seemed like even in a hospital the size of NYC Memorial, she was going to swim, and not sink.

"And you can call me Nicola, or Nic, either one."

"Okay, Nic, I should apologize for my attitude yesterday. I'm not used to people second-guessing me."

So she hadn't imagined it.

She gave him a smile. "I've been told by a very reliable source that I can be a bit abrasive at times."

His laugh was warm. "As someone who's also been called abrasive—and a few other things that aren't suitable for work—I can relate. You can be abrasive with me anytime you want. I promise to not be offended. Or at least try to get over it, if I am."

"I promise to do the same." She grinned. "Or at least try."

The door opened and Kaleb came in, glancing from one to the other. "I hope by the giddy look on both of your faces that this means good news for the patient. Was it a chalazion?"

Clint's eyebrows pulled together. "Now how on earth could you have guessed that?"

The scene in her office flew before her eyes, and stopped at the part where her head had been planted on his chest and his thumb had swept across her nape.

"Kaleb happened to be in my office, when I was going over the patient's files."

"But that wasn't in her files, or I would have seen it."

Kaleb came over and looked at the screen where Lindy's images were. "Nicola made a list of possibilities. And chalazion was on the top of her list."

Clint's eyes swung to hers. "So you figured this out, before you even asked the patient whether she'd had any problems with her eyelid."

"No, I hadn't figured it out. I just have this weird way of connecting lines on a diagram. Wherever most of those lines meet is the place I start looking first."

"And a chalazion fit all the criteria."

"It did. But I couldn't be sure unless the patient connected the dots for me."

Clint's fingers went to the computer screen and traced the small dot near Lindy's pituitary gland. "And if the patient hadn't remembered having that bump on her eyelid?"

"I don't know, honestly. All we can do is our best, using the information we have at the time."

Like telling Kaleb about Danny's suicide?

Like going to that bar and sleeping with him? Maybe. She'd done just what she said. Done the best she could to get by.

"So what's the treatment plan? Or is there one?" Kaleb asked. "If the patient's diplopia isn't caused by a tumor, can anything be done?"

"We need to get her vision stabilized so she can at least be fitted with glasses. So I'll be referring her to an ophthalmic surgeon. He may be able to deal with the scar tissue behind her lid and control whatever inflammation is still going on. But for now, we need to give the family the good news."

"We?" Nicola looked at him in surprise. Maybe he meant "we" in the figurative sense. Or maybe he meant for Kaleb to go with him.

He smiled. "I think since you're the one who actually made me second-guess my diagnosis, you should be there. And Kaleb, too, since he vouched for you."

Kaleb had vouched for her? That surprised her. Especially since he'd given her a little speech about playing nicely.

Well, not exactly that, but it was probably what he'd meant.

Her eyes met his and found him looking at

her, with one eyebrow quirked up. Ah, so he hadn't meant her to find out about that. But why? She'd do the same for him if need be.

"I'd love to go with you. Thank you."

Clint stood. "Kaleb, you in?"

"Sure. I'm always up for delivering good news."

But didn't he usually deliver good news? Well, the melanoma case certainly couldn't be considered good, but for the most part, he was helping someone feel better about themselves, right? So definitely not bad news, unless he was unable or unwilling to perform surgery on someone.

They made their way to the waiting room, where the family had been asked to stay until after the results were read. Lindy's dad stood first, looking worried. Who could blame him? They'd gone from thinking their daughter would undergo brain surgery, to them saying maybe not.

Clint went over and shook his hand then smiled at Lindy and her mom, who were sitting close together. "Well, I have some very good news, thanks to Dr. Bradley here. She—and I would agree—thinks the bump Lindy had on her eyelid changed the shape of her cornea and has caused her vision problem."

"So there's not a tumor?" Lindy's mom reached for her husband's hand.

"No. We don't think so."

"But the MRI…" she said.

"We're not sure what the image is, but we're pretty sure it's not a microadenoma, like I originally thought."

Lindy's dad sank back into his chair, still gripping his wife's hand. He lifted it to his mouth and kissed it, before looking at her. "This is great news. For all of us."

"Yes, especially since we want to add to our family. We were going to try, and then when Lindy developed double vision, we decided we needed to put it off to concentrate on her. But now I guess it's okay to move forward…?" She glanced up at Clint. "Right? Lindy's treatment isn't going to be complicated?"

"I don't believe so. There's a little pocket of scar tissue behind her eyelid that may need to be scraped to lower its profile, but it will almost certainly be a quick outpatient surgery. I'm going to call you with the number of a great surgeon who specializes in ocular problems. He should be able to do her surgery."

"How can I ever thank you?" Lindy's mom looked at Nicola, her eyes filling with tears.

"There's no need to thank me. I'm just happy it turned out to be something so simple."

"So are we." She hauled in a deep breath and blew it out. "So anything we need to do before we get your referral?"

Clint smiled. "Nope. Go and enjoy your life. And let me know how things go. Good luck on adding to your family."

Lindy's mom gave her husband a knowing look. "Thank you. And we'll definitely let you know about Lindy's treatment. Thank you again. All of you."

"Let me know if you need anything in the meantime. My office should call you sometime this afternoon with the information on the ocular surgeon. I'll touch bases with him, as well."

With that, they said their goodbyes and left the room.

"Well," Kaleb said. "These are the cases that make everything worthwhile."

"Agreed."

Kaleb looked at her and Clint. "Are you guys up for lunch at Plato's?"

"Not me, sorry." Clint said. "I'm supposed to meet with my wife at noon." He glanced at his watch. "And I'm about to be late. You guys go and enjoy." He left the room with a wave.

Nicola's stomach gave a twinge of protest. She was sure Kaleb hadn't been angling for lunch to be a two-person deal, so she tried to let him off the hook. "Look, I'm sure you have somewhere you need to be, as well."

"Yes, I do."

Nicola swallowed. He didn't have to be quite so quick to find an excuse. "Okay, well then, I guess—"

"I mean, yes, I do, as in I need to be sitting down to eat somewhere. You don't have to come, if you don't want to, but since it's noon…"

Maybe she'd feel better if she had something in her stomach. "That would be great. Is this place close?"

"It's actually just half a block from here. It's an easy walk."

"Okay, great."

They left the hospital and started down

the street. It was warm and muggy outside already, but at least the sun wasn't blazing down on them. Still, she was glad the restaurant was close, or she'd be wilting by the time they got there.

"Looks like you and Clint were on the same page this time."

"Yes, thanks to you." Nicola shifted to pass someone on the sidewalk. "Thanks for vouching for me."

He smiled. "I vouched for Clint, when I was talking to you, if you remember right."

That's right—he had. Some of the warm feelings she'd had about it melted away. So putting in a good word for her hadn't been so special after all. He probably did it with all of his colleagues. Part of his whole "collaborating" mindset.

"Well, I appreciate it, anyway, but don't feel like you have to stick up for me. Hopefully my work can stand on its own merit very soon."

"It already can. Except when two stubborn and proud personalities collide. I felt like a little mediation might be in order."

"Mediation. So you're a diplomat as well as a surgeon?" She couldn't totally banish the hint of irritation from her voice. Maybe it was the heat, but what had started off as something positive had shifted to feeling like he'd inserted himself where he hadn't been needed. "You don't think Clint and I could have worked it out on our own?"

He touched her arm. "Sorry. You're right. I wasn't trying to interfere. Danvers is a friend, but I certainly didn't want him biting your head off, since I felt you were onto something."

Okay, now she felt like a jerk. "I'm sorry. I'm just used to fighting my own battles."

"I know you are. I truly was just trying to help." His hand slid back to his side. "We're almost there. I hope you like burgers. Although they have some other things on the menu, as well."

"A burger sounds good right about now."

Her stomach was still a little rough, but she was pretty sure that as soon as she ate something, she'd feel better. That's what had happened this morning, although it hadn't lasted long.

Something pinged in her head, but she didn't have time to stop and examine whatever it was right now. If it was still there when she got home, she'd deal with it then.

A minute or two later they arrived.

Plato's had an artsy feel, with shiny chrome panels accented with touches of black. She admired the exterior while Kaleb went in to give their names. There were people waiting outside, but then again this was New York, so she shouldn't have expected anything else.

He came back out. "About fifteen minutes. Is that okay?"

"Better than I thought it would be, actually. I've heard of horrific wait times at some restaurants."

"There are a lot of people to feed in the city. You didn't have wait times where you were?"

"We did. But Grace Central was located a little off the beaten track, so it was easier to find an off time there."

He nodded, motioning her to some chairs that had been set outside under some nearby shade trees. "Do you miss it? Your old hospital, I mean."

"Hmm. That's a hard question. I miss the hospital itself. But I needed to make a change. Danny's death just cemented things. I'd also just gotten out of a relationship—with someone who also worked there—a few months before I applied at NYC Memorial. It…" She shrugged. "It was a hard time all the way around. And my hospital administrator felt like I needed to go somewhere with more opportunities. He's actually the one who found out the hospital here was looking for someone with a diagnostic emphasis."

"And you haven't looked back?"

She crossed her legs, searching for the right words. Her breakup, while hard, hadn't exactly been unexpected. But Danny's death…

While she did miss the smaller feel of her old hospital, it now held a lot of painful memories. And she'd come to realize her former administrator really was right. She thought she'd be leery of giving her opinions in a bigger hospital, but that hadn't been the case. She was still the same person she'd been before the move.

Then why didn't she feel the same?

"I've tried not to look back. Oh, I still have friends there that I miss, but I like it at NYC Memorial so far."

"I'm glad."

Was he? Was he really? She wasn't sure

why it mattered, but suddenly it did. Maybe a month and a half ago, she wouldn't have cared. But there was something about Kaleb that made her curious.

"I've told you quite a bit about myself. But I know almost nothing about you. How long have you worked at the hospital?"

"I actually came here fresh out of medical school. I can't imagine being anywhere else."

A man walked up, glanced at her with a tilted head and then greeted Kaleb. "Well, well, well. Funny to see you here."

"Hi, Snow. I could say the same about you."

Kaleb turned to her. "Snow, this is Nicola Bradley. She just started at the hospital a couple of weeks ago. She helped diagnose a case that Clint Danvers was working on. We're actually celebrating a good outcome, but Clint had somewhere he had to be, so he bailed on us."

Said as if he was trying to explain away eating lunch with her? Her stomach churned just a bit harder.

"Good outcomes are always reason to celebrate. You and I have had a couple of toasts about that very subject not too long ago." The man held out his hand. "Snowden Tangredi.

I'm one of NYC Memorials' transplant surgeons. Welcome to the hospital. You work with Clint?"

"Not exactly. I work in internal medicine, but specialize in diagnostics."

"Interesting. Kaleb and I go way back. You could say we've been through some memorable life events together. In fact—"

"Snow, she's not interested."

Actually she was. Intrigued was more like it, because Kaleb seemed to have known what his friend had been about to say and was anxious to head him off.

"Okay," Snowden said. "Although I'm not exactly sure that's true." The other man gave her a smile.

She had a feeling there was some pointed exchange happening between them that only the two friends could understand.

Nicola said, "We were just waiting to be seated. Do you want to join us? I'm sure we could add another person to our party."

"I'm not exactly sure Kaleb would like that." He shot his friend a look. "Besides, I'm headed to the courthouse to meet a friend—he's a lawyer there."

"Well, don't let us hold you up."

Kaleb's words were a bit sharper than necessary. She was right. Something was going on between these two that she didn't understand. But Kaleb wasn't anxious for his friend to stick around. It was almost as if he was hiding something and was afraid Snowden might spill the beans. But what?

She had no idea. But whatever it was, it was none of her business. So she let the men finish their small talk, only adding something if she was asked directly.

And when Snowden finally headed off in the direction of the courthouse, Kaleb seemed to relax in his seat.

And then they were being called by the hostess to head up front. Their table was ready.

And just in time to save Kaleb from answering any awkward questions. Not that she was going to ask them.

Even if she was dying to know what those life events Snowden mentioned were. And why Kaleb seemed so anxious to keep them quiet.

CHAPTER FOUR

NICOLA'S NAUSEA HADN'T gone away over the last week, and her period was still AWOL. It had put her in full-fledged panic mode. Which is why she'd been locked in the bathroom in her apartment for the last half hour, alternating between a false sense of calm and full-out panic. It was the moment of truth. She needed to know if her worry was justified.

And now she did.

Her professional self warred with her private self, each struggling to handle the news in her own way. Then she forced the diagnostician in her to work on the problem. What possible explanation was there—other than the most obvious one—for the two vertical stripes on the pregnancy test.

She swallowed as she stared at the indicator

in her hand. Okay…there was ovarian cysts. Kidney problems… Cancer.

But wasn't the most obvious reason also the most likely one, given the occurrences leading up to it? Especially since the test strip she was holding was the third one. With the exact same results.

She was pregnant.

God…pregnant!

The calmness swung back to terror. It had been almost eight weeks since that night at the bar. The night she'd tried to pretend hadn't happened. Or had at least pretended she'd been too drunk to remember. Situational amnesia.

Was that even a thing? Well, right now, she was wishing the amnesia was very real. Or that she at least had no idea who the father was.

That would be so much easier than what she was facing right now, which was telling Kaleb the truth.

Exactly how did she do that at this late date? Go to him and admit she'd been faking it all along? That she remembered every blasted second of that night?

Well, obviously she hadn't been faking

everything. But protection? God, yes, they'd used it. Each and every time.

Lining the plastic tests on the counter, she touched a finger to each one, the matching stripes telling a story she didn't want to believe. She wished she could sweep them into the trash and make this all go away. But she couldn't. She'd never really believed in fate.

Until now.

She was going to follow through with the pregnancy. Because the other option made her stomach churn in a way that had nothing to do with morning sickness. But that meant she wasn't going to be able to hide it from Kaleb. She would need prenatal care, sooner rather than later, since at thirty-five, the chances of chromosomal abnormalities went up, along with a whole slew of other things.

And Kaleb... God only knew how he would react to the news.

Her eyes met her own troubled gaze in the mirror, before glancing down at her body. There would be no disguising the changes that were heading her way. And even if there was, the baby would have to be born somewhere.

Just a week ago, she'd toyed with the idea

of starting a family. On her own. With some anonymous sperm donor. But this donor was far from anonymous. Far from a laundry list of defining characteristics with a carefully calculated timeline. And her vision of the procedure had been a hell of a lot chillier than her night with Kaleb had been.

It looked like the universe had taken the decision out of her hands.

Danny would probably find it amusing, that in trying to drown out what had happened that night at the hotel room, she'd actually created a reminder that would follow her for the rest of her life.

The image of Kaleb pushing a stroller teased her with might-have-beens that smacked of forevers and perfect endings. He would send her a look, eyes crinkling at the corners in a way that needed no spoken words.

There would be no looks, though. No spoken words.

Hadn't she gotten involved with a colleague once before? And where had that gotten her? Nowhere, that's where. She'd ended up leaving her previous hospital because of it. Well, not just because of it, but it had certainly played a part in her decision. In fact,

Bill had left first, before returning to the hospital a few months later. But by then, they'd both known there would be no going back.

No, Kaleb wasn't going to be in her life forever. But wasn't it okay for it to have happened this way? She respected Kaleb. Probably more than she should. And that laundry list she'd thought about moments earlier couldn't hold a candle to the flesh-and-blood man she could see. Had talked to. Worked with.

And the baby was definitely his—there'd been nobody else since Bill. There'd been nothing traumatic about their breakup, and Bill was a very nice guy. They'd simply decided they were better suited as friends than a romantic couple. The passion just hadn't been there. Soon after their breakup, he'd found that passion with a national-parks employee.

No. There'd been no one else. Hadn't even come close to sleeping with anyone.

She swallowed. Maybe Kaleb was right. Maybe she was too abrasive, pushing people away before they got close enough to hurt her. Ha! Leave before you got left.

Was that why she couldn't find love with someone, like Bill had, after their split? Because she held people at arm's length for fear that they would disappear?

Her hand swept from her neck down to her abdomen and rested there. Kaleb's baby might be growing inside of her, even now. She needed to tell him. Before it was too late and he accused her of keeping the news from him.

What if he'd been some faceless alcoholic, drinking his way to an early grave in that bar? Would she still feel the need to try to find him? To tell him he was going to father her child?

No. She wouldn't. And she was pretty sure if that had been the case, the person wouldn't want to be found.

So was it any more fair to Kaleb to tell him?

"He's going to find out, Nic. There won't be much hiding it, unless you call Bill and coax him to pretend the baby is his." But that wasn't fair to him, either, or his new girl-friend. Her hand pressed harder against her stomach, the earlier option coming back to her.

You could always just...

It would be easier, wouldn't it? No need

to tell anyone. Not her parents, not her colleagues and especially not Kaleb.

It would just be…gone.

A knife twisted in her midsection as she picked up the test again and stared at it. Pictured purposely erasing that extra vertical line. Pictured no birthdays. No Christmas celebrations. No future grandchildren.

"I can't. Oh, God, Kaleb, I'm so sorry, but I can't."

She wanted this baby. Already. In a way that defied explanation.

And Kaleb was a good person. People did this all the time, didn't they? Asked a friend or coworker to father their child?

It made for a good plotline in a movie or a book, but did it happen in real life? She had no idea.

But that ship had already sailed. She hadn't asked him to father a child. It had just happened.

And if she told him the truth… Well, would having a child be worth the horror of having to stand there and watch as Kaleb's face transformed from surprise to grim denial?

Yes, it would. That was temporary. Something that was uncomfortable in the moment, but that was adjusted to over a course of weeks or months. A new normal would somehow be forged.

And families were no longer just made up of a husband, a wife and their children. If Kaleb wanted to be involved in the child's life, she would make sure it happened. But for now, she'd explain that she hadn't done this on purpose and that she expected nothing from him in regard to the baby. But she owed it to him to at least give him the choice. The same way she was making the choice to have this baby. She also owed it to the baby to find out if there were any genetic issues that might need to be addressed down the road.

And if there were? Huntington's and a wide assortment of inherited disorders filed through her mind's eye. Well, she'd cross that bridge when she came to it. But first, she wanted to see Bill and ask him to run that test through the lab.

Bill? Was she seriously thinking of asking her ex to play a role in this? Why? Why not just find an ob-gyn at NYC Memorial?

She set down the test and thought about

their relationship. Despite the breakup, she trusted Bill. Knew him. Knew he would keep her secret. And he was a great obstetrician.

And since she had no idea how Kaleb was going to react when she finally told him, it made sense to have her pregnancy handled elsewhere. If he had a meltdown, it would be easier to have her appointments off-site, where she wouldn't have to face him and where news wouldn't somehow trickle back to him.

There was also her position at NYC Memorial to take into consideration. The timing wasn't the best, since she'd just started her job, and she was pretty sure Harvey might not be thrilled to find out that a doctor he'd had a hand in hiring might need to take maternity leave less than a year after her arrival.

Ugh! This was not going to be easy. On any front. And she'd have to tell her parents, although, honestly, that would probably be the easiest task of all. They'd be thrilled to be grandparents. She'd probably have to arm wrestle her own mother just to hold her baby. And maybe it would help ease a little of their grief over Danny's death. And hers.

"Well, baby, your timing may stink, but I want you to know you'll be loved. Very, very much. By the people who matter most." And maybe Bill would even consent to be the baby's godfather.

Speaking of Bill. She should call him sooner rather than later. Before she chickened out. So she washed her hands, abandoned the tests on the bathroom counter and made her way to the bedroom. Once there she sank on to the bed, picked up her phone and pushed the button listed by his name.

It rang twice and then a familiar voice answered. "Hi, Nic. Long time, no hear. How's the new hospital treating you?"

There was no awkwardness in the question. No stilted speech. And for that, she was grateful. It would make what she needed to ask a little bit easier.

"It's been good, so far." She gulped and then plowed ahead with her news. "So I think I may need your help with a slight problem. If you're willing, that is."

As soon as the words came out, a huge wave of emotion rolled through her, flattening her. Slight problem? No. It wasn't slight. It was a very, very big deal.

A life-changer.

Without warning, her eyes filled and a hic-cupped sob came out of her mouth. In the background she could hear Bill talking, the concern in his voice obvious. "Nic, are you okay? Hey, are you still there?"

But it was almost as if she was paralyzed and unable to respond, unable to do anything but sit there and try to catch her breath as a wave of dizziness swept over her.

Bill came back through. "Do I need to call 911?"

That got her attention. "N-no. No, sorry. Something's happened. Something I didn't plan."

"Don't tell me you're getting married?"

That got a strangled laugh. She was glad they'd been able to remain friends. "Hardly. I was told, in no uncertain terms, that I in-timidate people."

Those weren't exactly the words Kaleb had used, but the subtext had come through loud and clear.

"You? Intimidating?"

He drew the word out in a way that made her laugh again, her earlier panic beginning to uncoil. "Okay, so you've told me the same thing. I'm working on it."

"Hmm… I'll believe it when I see it." There was a pause and then he said, "Okay, Nic. If you're not involved with someone, then what's the problem? Trouble at the new job?"

"No, the job's fine." She cast around to find the words. Then once she found them, they came pouring out. "I think I'm pregnant, Bill. And I don't know what to do…"

"Pregnant? Are you sure?"

"According to the three home tests I took, I am."

There was a pause. "You need to come in and have it verified, of course."

"I know."

"You said you weren't getting married, and I assumed you weren't involved, but maybe I was wrong?"

It would be so much easier if she'd been like Bill, able to find true love on the heels of a broken romance. But she wasn't.

"No, you aren't wrong. I'm not involved. But I did have a night of…" Of what? Drunken debauchery? No. It hadn't been like that. "It was after Danny died. I went out and had one too many drinks."

"That's not like you."

No, it wasn't. And she was pretty sure it wasn't like Kaleb, either.

"I know. But it is what it is. And I need to make sure, before I say anything to the man I was with."

"So you're keeping it."

This was her chance to say no, she wasn't— that she couldn't raise a child on her own. And all of the other arguments that had run through her head.

"I think I am."

"And the guy? Do you care about him?"

"It's complicated. I actually work with him at the hospital, although I didn't know that at the time." It would have been so much easier if he'd just been a one-night stand, like she'd meant him to be.

"That makes it hard."

"I know. I'll figure it out somehow, though." She paused. "Will you take care of the testing part for me? I'd rather it not be here at NYC Memorial, if I can help it. I'll need to figure some things out before I tell the man in question. Or anyone else, for that matter."

"Well, congratulations… I think."

"Thanks. Like I said, it's complicated, and it wasn't planned, but I'm happy. At least right now. That may change in a matter of hours."

"Well, let me know when you want to come in. And you know I'll help with anything you need. Cheryl and I both will."

"Thanks, Bill, I really appreciate it." She paused. "How soon can you see me? As long as it won't complicate things with Cheryl."

"She'll be fine. I can do it this afternoon, if you want."

A wave of relief went through her. The sooner she knew for sure, the sooner she could plan her next move. "Thank you. I owe you one."

"No, you don't. The only thing you owe me is to be happy. If this is what you want, I'll back you one hundred percent. Can you get here around five? I'll just be getting off, so no one should be popping into my area to chat or ask questions."

"I'll be there. Thanks again."

Kaleb headed up the walkway and pushed through the door to the hospital just as some-one was trying to rush out. The person almost ran into him and skidded sideways to avoid him just as he realized who it was.

Nicola.

"Sorry," she said, eyes widening as she saw him, color sliding into her face and blazing across her cheekbones.

"You're headed somewhere in a hurry."

"I'm just getting off work and I'm running late. I, um, have an appointment in New Jersey."

His head tilted. She hadn't wanted him to catch her coming out, and she'd mumbled those last few words in a way that gave him pause. "You're not thinking of leaving us, are you?"

"Leaving? Why would I be...?" She shook her head. "Oh, my appointment. I am scheduled to meet someone at Grace Central, but it has nothing to do with my work here."

"Good to know." So who was she meeting? And why was that question even relevant? They'd had a good lunch the other day. Except for when Snow had appeared out of nowhere, looking far too interested in what he was doing there with Nicola. Kaleb wasn't exactly sure himself, and that bothered him. He'd forced himself to carry on like nothing out of the ordinary had happened, and they discussed cases and the differences between NYC Memorial and her former hospital. She'd said nothing about going there for an appointment. Or meeting anyone. But then at the end of their lunch, she'd suddenly gotten quiet, as if her thoughts had turned to something else. Something she didn't want to share. And he hadn't pressed. Because he'd had something he didn't want to share, as well. Namely his crazy pact with Snow, which he'd been fairly certain his friend had been about to blurt out.

She shifted her weight, making him realize he was standing there with the door open, blocking her way. He went back through it, holding it open. "Well, I'd better let you get on your way."

"Okay, thanks. I'll probably see you tomorrow."

Probably? Was she lying about leaving? She'd said she was happy at NYC Memorial, so it would be a sudden turnaround if that wound up not being the case.

"Okay, have fun."

She gave him a strange look before moving away from him. He watched her go, her steps quick and staccato, as if she couldn't wait to get to her destination.

Hadn't she said she'd been involved with someone at her old hospital? And that it had been part of the reason she'd left there? Maybe they were getting back together.

While that should make him feel relieved, somehow it didn't. Especially since they'd spent a pretty passionate night together.

Yes, and the woman didn't even remember it. It also didn't mean she couldn't go back to an old flame. Maybe they'd had a fight, or she'd caught him cheating and had wanted to retaliate.

None of that made him feel any better.

And if she did leave? That shouldn't matter to him at all. Unless Snow had noticed something that Kaleb had been oblivious to. Maybe he and his good friend should have a little chat.

Except the last thing he wanted to do was discuss Nicola with Snow…or anyone else, for that matter. He'd rather just power through this whole thing as if nothing was wrong.

Because it was true. Nothing was wrong.

Then why had he taken a woman he was supposed to have no interest in out for a meal?

Or stuck up for her with colleagues like Clint Danvers? Or sat in her office to "see what her process was"? He hadn't done that with any of his other coworkers. So why Nicola? Was it residual emotion from what had happened between them? If that was the case, he was in trouble. Deep trouble. Maybe Kaleb needed to take a step or two back and observe his behavior with an objective eye. The way Snow had.

And if he saw something he didn't like?

Then he needed to back away, while he still could. Before he found himself in another situation that would end badly, like with his exes.

Nicola was different. Although when he'd first seen her at the hospital, he'd wondered if she'd somehow known he worked at NYC Memorial the night they were together. And planned what had happened.

He'd later decided that wasn't the case. But in reality, he knew very little about the woman. He'd dated his former fiancée for more than a year and look at how little he'd known about her. And look at Snow. He'd known his wife for even longer and look where that had led.

No, he needed to tread carefully. Before he found himself sinking in quicksand, with no way out. And Snow standing on the banks saying "Don't look at me. I tried to tell you, and you wouldn't listen."

CHAPTER FIVE

NICOLA WAS STILL IN a daze the next morning. She'd already known in her heart of hearts that her little test strips at home had given her the correct response. She was pregnant.

Pregnant!

And Kaleb was the father.

Bill had been good enough not to ask about the specific circumstances beyond what she'd told him on the phone. And he'd also referred her to a colleague who was a newer ob-gyn at Grace Central. Treating her himself might be considered a conflict of interest, since they'd had an intimate relationship in the past. She hadn't thought about that, but he was right. So she'd walked out of the hospital with a card, for an appointment with her new obstetrician—a woman she'd never worked with, and who would hopefully ask no questions—next week.

And now she had to figure out when to tell Kaleb. Now, while things were early? Or after the first trimester, when there was less chance of miscarrying?

If she miscarried, it would be a moot point. Even the thought of that happening, though, made her throat squeeze shut.

She walked into NYC Memorial to start her new shift, heading to the coffee shop to pick up a cup of joe before going to her office and sorting through her appointments and consultations for the day.

Staring down at her phone as she stood in line, she tried to figure out if she should risk getting a bagel. Her stomach had been much better behaved this morning, even if her nerves were still a little shaky. A tap on her shoulder had her glancing back to see the very man she was thinking about.

She froze for a second or two, and she saw him frown as he studied her face. "Did your appointment not go the way you'd hoped it would?"

"Appointment?" Her voice ended on a squeak, then she remembered she hadn't specified whom her appointment was with. She took a breath. Then another. "Oh, that. Um, yes. It went fine."

Fine? Was that really the best word to use, if she was going to tell him about the pregnancy? He might think she'd somehow planned this.

No, that was crazy. It wasn't like she'd had an opportunity to sabotage the condoms they'd used. Plus, she'd never admitted to remembering that night. Although he'd never asked outright, so she hadn't had to make a choice about whether or not to outright lie about it.

And if he asked her exactly what her appointment had been about?

Maybe it was better to do this sooner rather than later.

Her heart became a racing, tripping thing in her chest. What if word somehow got back to him despite the HIPAA laws that were in place? Hospital grapevines were alive and well in most medical facilities.

If he was going to find out from anyone, she'd rather be the one controlling the narrative, right?

Yes. That in itself gave her the courage to open her mouth.

"Hey, I kind of need to talk to you about

something. Do you have any room in your schedule today?"

He looked at her for a second, and then someone behind them cleared his throat. Nicola realized she'd allowed a gap to form in front of her and it was now her turn. She moved forward and gave the cashier her order, then paid with her debit card. Kaleb did the same.

Once they had their orders, Kaleb said, "I have some time now. Do you want to find a seat?"

Oh, great. There was no way she was going to say the words "I'm pregnant and the baby is yours" here in the hospital cafeteria, where anyone could hear her. Where anyone could witness his reaction to the news. "Can we go back to my office instead?"

"That bad, huh?" He paused. "Let's go to mine. I need to check on something, anyway."

What could she say? That it wasn't bad news?

It might not be to her, but for him? Oh, yes, probably not news he would be thrilled to hear. But the sooner she got this over with, the sooner she could put this monster in her head to bed and stop obsessing over how he might react.

Then she could concentrate on the baby and not on the fear that her pregnancy might be discovered by him or someone else. Because he was absolutely going to guess, given the time frame.

"That sounds good. Thanks."

She followed him to the elevator and somehow endured the trip to the third floor. She hadn't realized his office was on the same floor as hers. When they got to the farthest corner of the building, Kaleb stopped to unlock a door.

Walking inside, she could see why the hospital administrator had said her office was pretty humble. Because Kaleb's was twice the size and had a sweeping view of the grounds. She guessed plastic surgeons brought in more revenue than a lowly internal-medicine doctor.

Not fair, Nic. For all you know, it goes by seniority and not specialty.

The office was furnished in dark woods and leather furniture, with a squashy couch flanked by two matching chairs to the left. A large screen on the wall behind the grouping must be to show his patients what they could expect from their procedure. It made more sense to have this in a reconstructive surgeon's office, anyway, since she could offer no before-and-after views. And someone like a urologist probably wouldn't need or want this kind of feature.

She caught him looking at her and realized she'd been staring at the television. "I'm taking it you consult with patients in here. Do before-and-after views?"

It gave her a funny feeling, like she was intruding on something intimate. Did he examine patients in here, as well?

That made her squirm, although she wasn't sure why. Her reasons for coming here flew out the window at the thought of a patient baring her breasts to him... Slowly walking toward him...

Dammit, Nicola, you're being ridiculous. He's a doctor. He's a professional. He has a job to do and he does it. Just like you.

"I do reconstructive surgeries. I'm not interested in face-lifts and augmentations, if that's what you're getting at." His voice was tight. Almost angry-sounding.

She blinked, realizing how out of line her

thoughts had been. "It wouldn't matter if you did. You would still be treating patients with a need, whether physical or emotional, wouldn't you?"

"Sorry. You're right. I'm not sure why I felt the need to say that."

"Plastic surgeons sometimes get a bad rap. I can see why it might make you defensive."

"Thanks, but I wasn't defensive. Just… cautious. Have a seat." He nodded at the grouping she'd been looking at.

Cautious? What did that mean? Lord, had he read her thoughts?

She did as he asked, now totally flustered. By his reaction to an innocent question. Oh, hell, she wasn't flustered by any of that. It was him. Just him. Kaleb had this presence that made her want to do exactly what she'd imagined moments earlier.

She'd purposely chosen one of the chairs rather than the sofa for just that reason, and she now perched on the very edge, cupping her coffee as if it could ward off the chill that was growing inside of her.

He sat on the sofa across from her and slid an arm along the back of the cushion, looking totally at ease. His dark-washed jeans and blue button-down shirt emphasized his lean good looks. And when that craggy line appeared in the side of his face... God, he was stunning. A real heartbreaker.

Only Kaleb hadn't broken her heart. Far from it. But at this point in her life and career, she neither wanted nor needed a relationship. If she did, she would have fought harder to salvage her relationship with Bill. They had both been focused on their careers, which had helped when they called things off.

And his biggest complaint had been that she was emotionally cool. Too cool. Maybe she was. She hadn't gotten Danny's effervescent personality and sharp wit. Although looking back, maybe those things had covered up a deep well of pain that no one knew existed. And his diagnosis might have brought it all to a head.

She swallowed and shook off the thoughts. She was at a new hospital, with brand-new opportunities to learn and grow. Even though she'd toyed with the idea of finding someone special, she wasn't desperate.

"So what did you want to see me about?"

See him about?

Her thoughts went completely blank for

several frightening seconds, before she blurted out the first thing she could grab hold of. "Um, well, before I came to the hospital, I was pretty sure I wouldn't know any of the staff here."

He leaned back, propping one ankle on his knee. His gaze was on her, sharp and wary. "And did you?"

She nodded. "Yes. It was a shock actually. So much so, that I didn't know what to say. Or how to react. Kind of like now."

"I know the feeling." That damn line appeared on the left side of his mouth. "Is this a confession, Nicola?"

"Kind of."

"So when Harvey introduced us, you did remember?" The words came out slowly, as if pondering the implications.

She nodded, her hands tightening on her cup. What else could she say?

"Hell, you sure had me fooled. I could have sworn you thought you were meeting me for the first time."

She paused, trying to find a way to mitigate some of the damage from her deception. Something that wouldn't present her in the worst possible light. If that was even possible at this point. "I thought it would make it super awkward if during that meeting, I said, 'Nice to see you again. I almost didn't recognize you with your clothes on.'"

"Ah, but you saw me with my clothes on. In the bar."

"Yes, but I wasn't paying attention to...*you.* Not until later."

"So it wasn't my witty dialogue that captured your attention." He leaned forward. "I had a feeling the bar scene wasn't someplace you normally found yourself."

How would he know that? Was it something *he* normally did?

"Definitely not someplace I normally go. Or something I normally do." She swallowed. They'd done some pretty damn sexy things.

"You seemed pretty...what shall I say?" The smile appeared again. "Uninhibited."

"Oh, God." She leaned back against the chair with an embarrassed laugh. "My only excuse is that I don't do a lot of drinking."

"So why were you drinking that night?" He paused, his eyes on hers. That mysterious line suddenly lost its grip on his face. "Ah, your brother?"

She nodded.

"Now it all makes sense. Strangely enough, I was there for the same reason."

"I don't understand."

He set his drink on the glass-topped table between them. "I'd just lost a patient."

"Oh!" Understanding dawned in a second. "The melanoma patient."

"Yes. No one expected her to go home and end her life."

"No one expected my brother to do that, either."

She needed to know. "And did it help? Going to the bar? Going back to the hotel?"

"Actually, it did. It was like it jump-started my system and helped me get back on track."

"Me, too." It hadn't erased the pain of what had happened, but it had helped her slide past it and start living again. Helped her realize there was still enjoyment to be found in life. For that, she would be grateful. "It was exciting. And dangerous. And just what I needed."

"I've never thought of myself as dangerous."

"Dangerous in a good way." The emotions of that night came back with a vengeance, bits and pieces of imagery filtering through her brain and reawakening the need she'd felt that night. Her eyes landed on his.

God. How could the man be so sexy, without even trying!

"My ego was pretty banged up when I saw you with Harvey, and you acted like you'd never laid eyes on me."

She laughed. "Harvey was there. And it seemed like the easiest solution at the time. And then afterward, I decided it was too late."

"So why say anything now?"

She hesitated. "Were you able to just shake off that night?"

"No."

The one word carried a wealth of meaning, and she found herself needing to moisten her lips. Tension crackled in the air between them as his gaze pinned her in place, making it hard to breathe. To think.

And then he stood, and her mouth went completely dry at the intent in his eyes. She suddenly wanted the warmth and sexiness he brought to the game. Needed it with a desperation that surprised her.

"No," he repeated. "I wasn't able to just shake it off. I still haven't."

He tugged her to her feet, his fingertips sliding into her hair.

Yes. This sexiness. This man had made her forget all her problems that night. "Me, either."

Almost as soon as the words left her lips, his mouth was on hers. A slow tasting that was so very different from the whirlwind of grief and need that had gone through her the last time they were together.

All thoughts were pushed to the remotest part of her brain. Because the only thing she wanted right now was to make this kiss go on for as long as humanly possible.

This time she could savor. Could enjoy the slight taste of coffee on his tongue, the friction of his lips as they moved across hers. Could revel in the way her emotions opened up and consumed her.

She should stop. Now. But her willpower was pretty much nil. The fact that he'd thought about her after that night, the same way she'd thought about him, was heady. Delicious.

Almost as delicious as his touch.

She hadn't realized the coffee cup was still in her hand, until she felt him take it. What happened to it after that was a mystery she wasn't interested in unraveling. All she knew was that she didn't want him to quit what he was doing.

With her hand now free, she could wrap her arms around his neck. The move pressed her fully against him, and her mind vaguely wondered how she measured up to patients he'd seen. To women he'd had before.

But it didn't matter. He wouldn't be kissing her like he was if there wasn't something about her that he liked. That made him want to tug her out of her seat and plaster his mouth to hers.

That was okay. Because there was something about him that held her captive, as well.

Suddenly he scooped her off her feet and strode to a small door at the back of his office. "Where are we—?"

"Twist the handle, Nicola."

She somehow coaxed her nerveless fingers to do his bidding, and the door opened to reveal a small bathroom, complete with sink, stool and shower.

"It's a little more private here," he murmured.

He pushed the door shut with his foot, then twisted the lock.

"Doesn't your office door lock?"

"Yes. But two layers of protection are better than one, don't you think?"

The words tickled at something in her head that was quickly forgotten when he set her down on the sink's countertop and cupped her face to kiss her again. He stopped for a second, looking at her. "How adventurous are you?"

He had no idea.

"Right now, I feel pretty damn adventurous."

"That's all I needed to hear, Nicola. Because I want you. Right now." His hands went to the edge of her skirt and skimmed it over her thighs.

She lifted to help, her pulse pounding in her ears. They were going to do it. Right here in his office. That's what he meant by adventurous.

And, God, she wanted him, more than any man she'd ever had.

"We don't have much time right now. But I'll make it up to you later."

Later? Her body turned warm as she imagined all the ways he might make it up to her. "Right now, I don't *need* very much time."

"You have no idea what you do to me."

She kind of did. Because he did the same to her. Only more.

He cupped her breast, thumb finding her nipple with the precision of a surgeon. That thought made her laugh.

"Something funny?" He squeezed lightly, turning her giggle into a low moan.

"N-no. Nothing." A feeling of breathlessness made it hard to think. Hard to speak.

She was drowning in a luscious vat of desire. One that she never wanted to climb out of.

Leaving her breast, his fingers looped in the elastic of her bikini panties and slowly peeled them down her legs.

Not much time. Not much time. The words repeated through her head, willing him to hurry. Because if something interrupted them, she was going to be a wreck for the rest of the day. She might have to find some quiet corner of the hospital and...

The sound of a zipper cut through her thoughts.

She gulped. No corner needed.

His arm curved around her butt and dragged her to the very edge of the counter.

He stepped between her legs, so she couldn't close them even if she wanted to. She definitely did not want to. A brief thought of protection came and went, but it was a moot point now.

Until a packet was pressed into her hand, and she felt him nudge her opening. "Do me, Nicola."

Oh, God. The bald words with their double meaning made heat arc through her belly and slide down to where he was waiting. Ready. So hot. So hard.

She used her teeth to tear into the plastic packet and took out the condom. She reached down, unable to touch him without her hand sliding over herself in the process. Her eyes closed for a second in utter ecstasy.

"I like that." His cheek brushed hers. "Here, honey. Let me help."

She felt his hand cover hers, and he sheathed himself. But when she went to move her hand away, he held it in place. "Let me help," he repeated.

His fingers cupping hers, he moved her to where she'd been moments earlier, right at the most sensitive part of her body. He used her fingers to stroke herself, and the utter sensuality of it made her teeth come down on her lower lip. She had to stop herself from crying out. She moaned instead.

"Do you feel it, Nicola? This was what it was like for me that night. You are so soft. So sensitive. It drove me wild."

It was driving her pretty wild, too. His erection brushed between their hands, and he included it in their play, gripping it as he continued to urge her to stroke herself. And when her eyes came up, she found him watching her.

"You are absolutely gorgeous. Your pupils tell me everything I need to know."

He moved her hand for a second and entered her with a hard thrust that drove the breath from her lungs. He groaned against her ear. "Touch yourself, Nic. I want to feel you."

She couldn't resist him if she wanted to. Wrapping her legs around his hips to hold him in place, she did as he asked, the combination of what she was doing along with the deep purposeful movements inside of her making her world spin out of control. Her lids fluttered closed.

"No, baby. Open those beautiful green eyes. I want to see the moment it happens."

She struggled. Tried and failed the first time. But, somehow, she parted her lids. Focused on him as one hand slid up her back and buried itself in her hair. He tipped her back, supporting her with his arm, and then bent over, took her nipple in his mouth and sucked hard.

"Ah…" This time she couldn't stop herself from crying out as a cliff rushed forward to meet her and whispered for her to jump. His tongue lapped her, the movements in time with her stroking fingers, and suddenly it was too much. She took off over the edge, colors swirling as she sailed out into space, her body spasming around him.

She felt him pumping like a wild man, and then he suddenly stiffened, everything coming to a complete halt for several long seconds.

Then he relaxed, pulling her back up to rest against him, his breathing ragged.

She wrapped her arms around his back and held him there, not wanting to come down. She'd never had that kind of reaction before, had never been so totally lost in the act. Not even last time at the hotel. At the time, she'd thought it was the highest of highs. She couldn't have been more wrong.

He kissed her shoulder. "I really don't want this to be a wham-bam thing, but I have a patient I need to see."

"It's okay." She unhooked her legs to let him move away, which he did, making a face as he slid free.

Discarding the used condom, he zipped himself back in, then reached down to scoop up her panties. When he tugged them up her legs, a strange surge of emotion come over her. Had to be hormones.

Hormones!

Oh, God, she'd almost completely forgotten. Actually she had forgotten during the last part of their time together. She hopped off the counter and pulled her undergarment back into place, tugging her skirt down, as well.

"What was it you wanted to tell me?"

Had he read her mind? She swallowed hard, bile washing up her throat. What had she been thinking? She'd come here to tell him something important, not have sex with him. Again.

But if she didn't say it now, she was going to chicken out and put it off. And it would just get more and more complicated with each passing day. Especially if they slept together again, like he'd hinted.

"I'm sorry, Kaleb. This is a little different from how I'd envisioned this scene, and I'm not sure exactly how to say this." There was a long pause. One in which his carefree attitude seemed to dry up and a wariness infused the muscles of his face.

"So you *are* leaving."

"No. No I'm not, but you might wish I was when you hear what I'm about to tell you." She licked her lips and forced herself to say the words that would change both of their lives. Forever.

"I'm pregnant."

CHAPTER SIX

"No, you're not. You can't be."

"Excuse me?"

He'd heard what she'd said, but it made no sense at all. Unless… "Okay, maybe I missed something. You're pregnant, but who's the—?"

"Don't." She held up her hand, a flash of anger crossing her face. "Don't even try to do that."

His brain hadn't fully recovered from what they'd just done, but of all the things she could have said, "I'm pregnant" had not even been on his radar. "We just now had sex, and we used protection. There's no way you can claim to be carrying our child without sounding totally crazy."

Maybe she was crazy. Had she wanted to meet in one of their offices for just this purpose? To have sex and then say she was pregnant? Why? Did she want something from him?

His ex-fiancée's desire to marry a plastic surgeon spewed back into his mind. But as bad as that was, she'd never pretended to be pregnant to get what she wanted.

It made everything he'd done with Nicola seem tainted now. When he thought of what he'd said. Of what they'd done...

"Sorry to disappoint you, Kaleb. But even your sperm doesn't wear a Superman cape and make me magically aware of the moment of conception. I did a pregnancy test at home several days ago that came back positive. And my appointment was with a friend in New Jersey to confirm the news." Her lips tightened. "It's from that night at the hotel. Not today."

The pieces fell into place with a thump that made his head rattle. Hell, how could he not have figured out what she was trying to say? That's why she'd seemed so strange when she left the hospital.

She was pregnant. And it was his baby. So why had she had sex with him just now?

Unless she was softening him up. Manipulating him, hoping to get the reaction she wanted.

His ex had used sex, too, right before asking him do a little work on her face.

"Did you plan to have sex with me? Is that why you wanted to go back to your office rather than talk somewhere in the open?"

"No!" She cleared her throat before continuing. "No, of course not. And this shouldn't have happened at all. It's just that I knew once I told you… Never mind. I'm sorry. Truly I am. And I don't expect you to do anything about the baby. I just felt like you should know. And you were bound to figure it out, since Immaculate Conception hasn't happened in a very long time."

"The baby." His brain latched on to those two words. "So you're keeping it."

"I am. I'm sorry if that makes you uncomfortable. I'm not planning on telling anyone who the father is. I'll even leave you off the birth certificate. I just didn't want you to put two and two together and start asking awkward questions."

"This goes a little beyond awkward, don't you think? How did this happen, anyway?"

She gave a laugh that sounded pained.

"How does it normally happen? It starts off with a man and a woman doing what we did here in this bathroom."

"Hell. And I need to be somewhere in fifteen minutes. We need to talk. Outside of the hospital this time."

"There's no need. Like I said, I don't expect anything out of you."

He felt like an idiot now. He'd suspected all kinds of nefarious motives that had no place in reality. Who was crazy now?

"Well, *you* might not expect anything, but I expect something from myself. This is my child. And I'd appreciate not being cut out of his or her life." His anger flared, but this time at himself. At the way he'd just dragged her into the bathroom as if he had no self-control at all. Maybe he didn't. Not where she was concerned. After all, hadn't he cuddled her close in that hotel room, as if there was something more between them than sex? And he wasn't quite sure what to do with that thought.

He and Snow had made a pact, dammit. One that he knew was for the best.

And yet here he was, expecting a child with someone he didn't love. It was crazy to be expecting a child with *anyone*, for that matter. He didn't have the picture-perfect marriage that his parents had and probably never would. His track record in that department was so seriously flawed it was laughable. This latest foray just drove that point home.

This poor kid.

But it was what it was. There was a baby, and along with the reality that was staring him in the face came responsibility. A responsibility he couldn't turn his back on. Nor did he want to. If Nicola was having this baby, he was damn well going to make sure the child had a father he could be proud of. No more acting like nothing could touch him. No more dwelling on that damn pledge between him and Snow.

He was going to play a part in this baby's life. A big part. Whether Nicola wanted him there or not.

She told you about it, didn't she? That had to account for something.

"Meet me after work, and we'll go somewhere and talk."

"There's no need to—"

"Yes, Nicola, there is. And if you think otherwise, you're very much mistaken. This baby is going to grow up with a mother *and* a father."

She stiffened. "I'm not getting married."

"Then that makes it easier." He gave a hard smile, ignoring the inference in her words. If she could pretend she didn't remember their first night together, he could damn well pretend he didn't understand. Because she was right. She wasn't getting married. Not to him, anyway.

The vision of her standing in a wedding dress smiling at some man who wasn't him made his gut twist sideways. But he'd better face facts. To marry her without love would only be setting them both up for disaster. Or for an ending like Snowden's marriage. His wife had cheated on him and then filed for divorce. There was no way he was putting a child of his through that. So no marriage. Not today. And probably not ever. But there had to be other ways of making sure their baby knew his father loved him or her.

But would he even be able to love a child?

At the thought of a baby, cradled in his arms, his gut shifted again. Along with his heart. Yes, he would. He was sure of it.

As if reading his thoughts, her eyes moistened and she turned away. "I'm so sorry, Kaleb. I didn't plan for any of this to happen."

Of course, she hadn't. And he had been a royal jerk. He went over and cupped her arms, his thumbs stroking her soft skin. He didn't dare hug her. "I know. I'm not sure quite how this came about, but we'll get through it. We'll figure out how we're going to handle the prenatal appointments, the birth and what comes afterward."

"Prenatal?" Her face went very still. "Oh, but—"

"We can talk about it after work." He glanced at his phone. "I really do need to go, before my patient wonders what happened to me. What time do you get off?"

There was a pause, and at first he thought she wasn't going to tell him. Then she closed her eyes. "I get off at six."

"I get off at five thirty. I'll do a little work in my office while I'm waiting for you."

"You want me to meet you…here?"

He glanced around. That was so not a good idea. Especially after all that had happened. "I think it's better if we do this in a more neutral setting. Maybe one of the parks."

"Okay." The relief in her voice was obvious. "I'll meet you just outside the hospital at six fifteen, okay? It'll give me time to change into some jeans and sandals."

That was probably a good idea, since her skirt had been far too convenient. Plus, seeing her in it would immediately bring up images he needed to file away for good. "All right. I'll meet you at the west exit. The one you left through to go to your appointment." Lord, that seemed like forever ago, when in reality it had been just yesterday. And he'd gone from thinking she might be leaving NYC Memorial to finding out he was going to father a child.

His world was pretty much in shambles right now. But as soon as he had time, he was going to sit down and figure out how to put it all to rights. At least he hoped that was possible. Because if not, it was going to be a very rough nine months. "You can stay in the office for as long as you need to."

Right now, he needed to be anywhere but here. So with a quick wave, he headed out.

Waiting impatiently for the elevator doors to open, he pushed the button again. When they did, they revealed the last person he wanted to see right now. Snow. And unfortunately, his friend was the only one in the elevator.

"Just the man I've been looking for."

"Not in the mood, Snow. I'm already late for an appointment with a patient." And he definitely did not want to get into why he was late. Not to mention the aftermath of that 'why' with its accompanying revelation.

"That's okay, I'll ride down with you." His friend grinned, completely ignoring what Kaleb had just said. "Interesting woman at the restaurant with you the other day. She's new here, isn't she?"

His jaw tightened enough to send a spear of pain through his skull. "Yes. And don't get any ideas." At least not yet. Not until he'd had a chance to sort through all of this and figure how to best deal with things. And he knew without a doubt that Snow was going to have an opinion or two of his own, once news of the pregnancy got out. Right now, though, he couldn't deal with seeing his friend gloat. Or offer words of condolence that would make him feel even worse about the situation. Nothing was going to make this go away, so right now, he just needed time, and lots of it.

"I'm not getting any ideas. I was just curious about how you met her. I'd never seen her before that day at the restaurant. And you're not exactly a social butterfly."

No, he wasn't. And that was definitely not a story he was going to get in to. "Nothing to be curious about. Harvey introduced us, since I happened to be there when she was getting the grand tour."

That was actually the truth, since Harvey had indeed made those formal introductions. And the less formal ones?

Well, those were not something he was going to talk about. Not to his friend. Not to anyone, if he could help it. Kaleb had no idea what Nicola had told her friends or relatives. And right now, he didn't care as long as none of them knew Snow personally.

The elevator came to a stop and Kaleb got off. Unfortunately, so did Snow. "Any chance we could meet up for drinks after work?" his friend said.

Since he was supposed to be meeting Nicola, he didn't think so. "I can't tonight."

"Hot date?"

That made him stop and glare at his friend. "No date at all. I just have some stuff to do, that's all."

Like figure out how he and Nicola were going to make this whole thing work.

"Okay. No need to get all hot under the collar about it."

"Sorry. It just hasn't been a good day. How about Friday or Saturday for drinks?"

"Either of those works, since unlike you, I don't have any special plans. Then again, we both agreed that was something we wouldn't miss, right? The dating? The relationships?"

"Right."

So how did he explain to his friend that while he might have technically kept the terms of their toast, he'd had sex with the newest member of NYC Memorial's staff? Not once, but twice. And had fathered a child with her. Hell. He couldn't even explain it to himself, much less anyone else. At least not right now. Not until he'd had a chance to sit down with Nicola and come up with a plan they could both agree on.

And right now, he was at a loss as to how that was even possible. How any of it was possible. Other than to say that she'd some-how bewitched him and made him forget that he was a rational man who was supposed to have had a rational new outlook on life. And love.

Not that love was involved here. At all. And when Nicola had mentioned marriage, the feelings of how things had been with Melanie—and then after her, Candice—came roaring back. The slyness. The hints. Thank God Mel had never gotten pregnant, or the split would have been that much harder. And Candice... Well, she'd been looking for something in addition to love.

But Kaleb was no longer under the pressure of medical school the way he'd been when Melanie wanted to start a family. So maybe now wasn't such a bad time to have a baby.

But with Nicola? He pulled up outside of one of the exam rooms. "Well, this is my stop. Let me know when you want to have those drinks."

"How about tomorrow? Seven at our usual place."

"Let's try somewhere new." Kaleb didn't know why, but he didn't want to go back to the bar where he'd met Nicola. Not with the way things were right now.

"Okay. How about that place in east Manhattan. I'm too old to go clubbing."

"Define old." He said it with a strained grin.

"Too old to stay out until two when I have to be back here at five in the morning."

That he could definitely relate to. "Okay, east Manhattan it is. I'll meet you at the bar on the corner of Sunset and Brewer."

"Sounds good." Snowden headed down the hallway.

Giving himself a moment or two to regain his composure, Kaleb finally pushed through the door to meet his first patient of the day. Or he should say his patient's parents, since the person he was actually here to see was an infant who'd been born with a cleft lip.

As he took in the scene, he found a very young man and woman sitting in the two seats in the exam room. The man was holding a wrapped bundle. The sight made his chest squeeze. Why did he have to be dealing with a baby, now of all times?

Kaleb forced a friendly smile. "Hello, I'm Dr. Sabat. You must be Mr. and Mrs. Taylor?"

"Yes. Jim and Terra. And this is Trey."

Trey.

If he and Nicola had this baby, what would they name him or her? Would he even be given a chance to help decide?

He set the chart on the bed and peered down at the swaddled baby, the squeezing in his chest growing tighter.

He needed to get his mind back on his job, for his patient's sake. He tried to look at the baby in terms of the cleft defect, which was clearly visible on the right side of the infant's face. According to the chart, the hard palate wasn't affected, just the lip. It would be a fairly straightforward repair. He would just have to make sure he lined the lip margins up perfectly. It might not be noticeable now, but any deviation would become obvious as the child grew and the skin on his lips stretched.

Trey's mom looked at him. "Can this be fixed? I don't want anyone to…" Her voice cracked and she had to try again. "I don't want anyone to make fun of him."

He could well understand her fear. And it was his job to help quell any fear. And in this case it was easy to give reassurance.

"Babies have a remarkable ability to heal. If all goes well, in six months this will be barely noticeable. Maybe a slight redness as the scar heals. But by the time he starts school? It will be a very narrow white line. Certainly not something his peers will notice when they're out on the playground. On the off chance there is a problem, we can do revision surgery a little bit later."

Jim Taylor looked at him for a long time, a muscle in his jaw working, then he spoke. "Is Trey paying the price for being...unplanned?"

Shock went through him, and Kaleb had to work hard to make sure neither of his parents saw it. "Of course not. This was a simply a glitch that happened during cell division. Your baby is going to be fine." He normally didn't give reassurances like this, because nothing was ever certain when it came to surgery, but the baby's dad seemed so beaten down by guilt that Kaleb hadn't been able to help himself. "I'm sorry if someone told you that."

"No," Terra said. "No one said that, but when I first got pregnant..." She closed her eyes. "I didn't want the baby. It was only a couple of weeks later, when I'd decided against getting an abortion, that I allowed myself to care for him. Maybe my rejecting him ended up doing something to him. Maybe it caused that 'glitch' you talked about."

While there were certainly studies that seemed to indicate that high levels of stress early in pregnancy could play a part in some types of birth defects, cleft lip being one of those, the stress would have to be something sudden and profound to disrupt development.

"That's highly unlikely, Terra. I wouldn't worry about that. And Trey's lip should be easy to repair."

It made him think, though. It had to have been stressful for Nicola to tell him about her pregnancy. Were damaging hormones even now flooding her system? He needed to make sure he didn't add to her stress, even though what he'd said was true, that it was unlikely anything he said or did would contribute to his own baby having developmental challenges. And he was pretty sure she would be furious if he treated her with kid gloves.

Pulling up a stool, he said, "Let's take a look." Taking the baby from his father, he laid the infant on his lap, tummy facing up to do a mini exam of his own. Blue eyes stared up at him, blinking as they did an examination of his own. "Hey there, little one. How are you?" He touched a finger to the baby's nose, a feeling of longing going through him. Would he hold his own baby like this, their eyes studying each other?

Swallowing and trying to corral his wayward emotions, he took his stethoscope and listened to Trey's breathing, and especially to his heart, since sometimes cardiac problems accompanied cleft lips and palates. But everything looked and sounded good.

"He's had an EKG, has he not?"

"Yes. His pediatrician said his heart was normal. His lungs are good, too. It seems to be just his lip and nothing else."

Just his lip and nothing else.

Something rattled around in the back of his head. His melanoma patient had thought she just had a deviated septum. Simple. Easy fix. What if this wasn't as cut-and-dried as it looked? What if he was giving them an assurance that didn't match the situation?

Where was this uncertainty coming from?

Maybe because now he was expecting a baby of his own. What if he was in the situation these parents were? Wouldn't he want the doctors to check and double-check until there was no other possible answer?

Lines that all culminated in a single diagnosis.

Like the ones that Nicola drew for herself.

Maybe he should call her in on this case, just to be sure.

"That's good news." Kaleb studied the lip, taking measurements of the length and position of the gap. "Any problems suckling?"

He needed to figure out how to broach the subject of Nicola coming to examine the baby without worrying the parents any more than necessary. Especially since under normal circumstances he wouldn't have asked for another consult. The baby's pediatrician had cleared him. Wasn't that enough?

Not right this second, it wasn't.

"No problems. He seems to have figured out what to do."

Since the palate wasn't affected, there wasn't the problem of having fluid traveling into the baby's nose instead of being swallowed. "That's also good. Once the lip is repaired, nursing will be even easier, on both of you."

"How many stitches will he need?"

"I can't give you an exact number. We'll do the sutures in sections. We can't just sew up the outside, because it would still leave a gap behind the lip. So we normally do the stitching in layers. One layer in the back. One in the middle, and then the final stitches on top, where the repair will be the most visible."

"How soon can Trey have the surgery?" Jim asked.

"Let me look at my schedule. I'd also like to call in a colleague to look the baby over, if that's okay."

"Is something else wrong?" Mrs. Taylor asked.

"I'm not seeing anything else, but I would just like another set of eyes to make sure we don't miss anything."

She glanced at her husband and nodded. "We want that, as well."

"Let me call her and see if she's available. I'll be right back."

He handed the baby back to Jim and stepped into the hallway. Dialing her number, he put the phone to his ear. The second her voice came across the line, his gut clenched. What was he doing here? Was this about Trey? Or about talking to the mother of his child?

"Hi, Nicola, are you busy?"

"Aren't we meeting later?"

There was no irritation in her voice, just puzzlement. "Yes, but I have a patient that

I'd like you to take a look at, if you have a few moments."

"Yes, of course. I'm just in my office writing up some notes. Where are you?"

He had no idea. Somewhere between stupid and clueless. "I'm down in Pediatrics, room five."

"It's a child?"

"Yes."

Before he could tell her the details, she said, "On my way," and then hung up.

He entered the room again, still holding his phone. Flipping to his calendar, he saw he was pretty booked up, meaning he might need to put off his drink with Snow until another time. Which didn't make Kaleb unhappy. And at least his friend would understand him canceling due to a patient, whereas if he put off their trip to the bar due to going somewhere with Nicola... Well, Snow would probably ask questions he'd rather not answer.

"My colleague will be here in a few minutes, so let's talk dates. I think I can work you into my surgical schedule tomorrow or Saturday, how's that?" Insurance had already preapproved the surgery, so they wouldn't need to wait for that.

"Would Saturday work? I'm pretty sure my mom and dad will want to fly in for the surgery." Terra glanced at Jim, who nodded.

"Saturday afternoon will be great, if my colleague concurs. I'll call it in and if there are any scheduling conflicts with the surgical suites, I'll let you know later this afternoon."

A knock at the door signaled Nicola had arrived. "Come in."

She came in, hair now pulled back in a ponytail with tendrils trailing the sides of her face. She looked clean-faced and far too beautiful. This was probably a huge mistake. But he wanted to be sure.

"Dr. Bradley, this is Mr. and Mrs. Taylor."

Nicola shook hands with both of them. When she saw the bundle, her eyes widened.

Mrs. Taylor must have noticed, because she said, "This is Trey."

Lowering herself into the chair next to the baby's mom, the diagnostician reached her arms out for him. "May I?"

Settling the wrapped infant in the crook of her arm, she looked far more comfortable holding the baby than he'd felt.

She looked down at the infant and smiled, and hell, that smile…

It was real and warm, with a softness unlike anything he'd seen in her. The image of her holding their baby like this swam behind his eyes. Gorgeous. Why had he said marriage was out of the question?

Because it was. She didn't love him. And even when love was present, things didn't always work out.

But sometimes they did. Like his parents' marriage. And his sister's.

You're not your parents or your sister. You've tried twice and failed.

"Hi, Trey. You're a big, handsome boy," Nicola crooned, her voice a melodic blend that perfectly blended comfort with reassurance. He watched as Mrs. Taylor visibly relaxed. Kaleb wasn't sure what she expected, but whatever it was, the other woman seemed relieved.

So was he. This wasn't a mistake. At least not as far as the baby was concerned.

How about as far as he was concerned?

Well, the jury was still out on that one.

Nicola's finger traced Trey's lip, then she angled the baby up and uncoiled her stethoscope, doing her own listening before nodding. "I like what I'm hearing."

Unfortunately, so did Kaleb.

She continued, "I haven't studied his chart yet, but I'll do that in a bit, but are you okay if I ask you a few questions?"

"Of course," said Mr. Taylor. "Anything that will help."

She handed the baby back to his mother and pulled out the sketchbook. The one that held her brother's page in it. He was surprised she hadn't started a new book after his death. But maybe it was a reminder of what to look for. What could happen.

She asked about the pregnancy, touching Mrs. Taylor's hand when she talked about not wanting the baby as the woman related the same story she'd told Kaleb. "That must have been hard. But it's very obvious you love your baby. And nothing you did caused that. That's not what I'm looking for. I just want to make sure that surgery goes as planned without any surprises."

"That's what we want, as well."

Nicola was busy drawing her boxes and filling them in, leaving the extra ones blank. A few minutes later, she closed the book. "I think I have all I need. Let me review the chart and see if I find any surprises, given what you've told me. I'll have Kaleb… Dr. Sabat notify you if I see any areas of concern."

"Thank you. We appreciate you coming down on short notice."

"It's not a problem. I was happy to come." She glanced at Kaleb. "Can I get those charts from you?"

"Yep, let me get them from the nurse's station."

"Okay." She glanced at the parents. "I'll say goodbye for now. And congratulations on your baby. He must bring you a lot of happiness."

"Yes, he does."

With that, Kaleb and Nicola went into the hallway.

"I don't see anything out of the ordinary. Were you concerned about something?"

Did he tell her he was suddenly afraid of missing something? Or just lie and pretend that asking for a second opinion was routine?

He decided to go with the truth. "I find myself second-guessing myself sometimes. Because of my other patient. I just wanted to see what you thought."

"Me, too."

"Sorry?"

She sighed, tucking her sketchbook under her arm. "I find myself afraid of missing something important, too. Especially after what happened to my brother."

She understood. Had felt exactly what he had.

"It's hard."

"I know." She glanced down the hallway. "I didn't realize your patient was a baby."

Something in her voice told him that she was feeling the same thing he had when he'd looked into that infant's face.

"It makes it different when you have one of your own coming, doesn't it?"

She nodded. "It does. It's hard not to put myself in their shoes and wonder what I would do. It makes me want to check and double-check the findings."

"Yes. Which is exactly why I called you in."

"I'm glad you did." She smiled, and although the curve of her lips wasn't quite as high as the one she'd given the baby, it still hit him in the solar plexus.

"I'll email you the charts, if that's okay?"

"That's fine. Are we still meeting after work?"

"I would like to, yes."

"Okay, then I won't hold you up." She hesitated. "I'd like to observe the surgery, if I could."

That shocked him. She wanted to watch him work? Or was this about the baby, more than it was about him. Yes, of course it was. There was no way it came out of any kind of interest over his surgical strategies.

"That's fine. There an observation area over all of the surgical suites except for number three. I haven't called to reserve a room yet, but when I do I'll let you know where to come."

That didn't sound quite right. It almost sounded like he was reserving a hotel room rather than a surgical room.

"All right. That sounds good. I'll let you know at the park if I find something else in the charts."

"Okay, thanks. See you later."

He watched as she turned and walked down the hall, her back straight, hips softly swaying.

He knew one thing. He really hoped he was

in any room other than surgical room three. He could handle her watching from a distance, but to be in the same room with him? That would be something he'd rather not do.

To keep from staring at her, he swiftly turned and walked back into the room to say his goodbyes to Mr. and Mrs. Taylor.

"Okay, she's going to call me later and tell me what she thinks."

"Thank you so much. You don't know how much this means to us. One of my coworkers said you were the best in the area. He has a friend who split his head open in a motorcycle accident. You did his surgery, and he said the scar is barely visible."

Kaleb was pretty sure he remembered that case. It had taken over a hundred stitches to coax the skin to cover the repaired skull fracture. But the outcome had been a good one.

"We'll get Trey fixed up."

"Thanks again. We're so happy you were here when we needed you."

Kaleb was, too. Once the shock had worn off over seeing his tiny new patient, working with the parents had helped take a little of the edge off. Nicola's pregnancy revelation coming on the heels of having sex with her had done a number on him. But it was neither of their faults. It had happened. And it was their new reality. Both his and Nicola's. What they did from here would lay the groundwork for all their future interactions. So these first few weeks needed to be carefully managed.

If his parents could survive raising him and his sister, surely he could survive having a baby of his own. Couldn't he? He and Nicola might not be together in the way his mom and dad were, but they could be together in a different way, couldn't they? They could be united in purpose, even if they weren't necessarily united in matrimony. So, yes, carefully managed. That was the name of this particular game.

The shade was heavenly this time of summer. And the walk through Central Park to get here hadn't been bad, either. Nicola had been right. The relief she'd felt for the rest of the day after laying her news in front of Kaleb had been wonderful.

Maybe not quite as wonderful as the sex had been, but that part had been a mistake. It would have been a whole lot less complicated to have told him without worrying about their attraction getting in the way.

And it was attraction. She could admit that. Their first time together could be blamed on the alcohol and heightened emotions that loss had brought to the table.

But the time in his office? No. That tension had been crackling since the moment they sat down. She'd thought it would be okay. That she needed to feel him next to her one last time.

But the horror on his face afterward—when he finally realized what she was trying to say to him—had been pretty unmistakable. And it had been pretty unshakable, as well. It had followed her into the room when she'd done her examination of Trey. She'd felt his eyes on her as she'd looked over the tiny infant, and tried to hide the shock of tender emotions that had gone through her.

She looked for signs of the horror from earlier in his face now, but she was having a hard time reading him.

"I'm going to get us a couple of drinks. What would you like?"

"Sweet tea. Or lemonade if they don't have that. But I can come with you."

"Why don't you wait here and save our places on the bench. And then we can talk about Trey's case and...that other thing."

That other *thing*? Wow, the horror might not be in his face for all to see, but she was pretty sure it was in his voice. In his thoughts. "Okay."

As he headed down the path to the vendor across the way, she sank onto a nearby bench. At least she had a few minutes alone to try to compose her thoughts. She'd opted to drive here separately so she could go straight home afterward. And to reduce the awkwardness of being together under these circumstances.

Someone whizzed by on a bicycle, helmet buckled in place looking like he had somewhere to be. Or maybe he was training for an upcoming race. Whatever it was, the rider looked carefree and relaxed. The opposite of what she felt right now. While she was relieved that Kaleb knew the truth, she wasn't quite as relieved that he hadn't simply said, "Do what you want. It's nothing to do with me."

That would have been the easier road. One where she made all the decisions for her child

without any interference from him or anyone else.

Instead, he'd insisted he wanted to be a
part of this baby's life. *His* baby's life. He
did not want to be just a sperm donor. Which
was why Nicola was experiencing a mixture
of dread and excitement. Dread that Kaleb
would be in her life despite the fact that he
turned her insides to mush and made her want
to drag him back to her apartment and eat
him up. And not the sexual kind of excitement that was part of her "dread" statement,
but excitement that her baby would have a
father who wanted to be involved.

Those two emotions were vying for top
spot, but so far there was no clear winner.
It changed from day to day, from minute to
minute. Right now the needle was pointed
toward the excitement part of the equation.

She saw Kaleb returning. And sure enough,
he was carrying two cups.

He sank on to the bench next to her, handing her one of the cups. "They did have sweet
tea."

"Perfect, thanks. I'll need to be careful
with what I eat soon enough. But for today?
Sweet tea sounded wonderful. What'd you

get?" Since it was illegal to drink alcohol in any of New York's parks, it probably wasn't beer.

"Lemonade."

That surprised her. Although she wasn't sure why.

One side of his mouth quirked. "There was a kid in the booth who talked me into a glass. Said he was raising money for a camping trip with a boys club."

Okay, so that didn't surprise her. But it did touch her. "I would have helped him, too."

"Well, since sweet tea was your first choice, I decided to stick with what I knew."

That just emphasized how little they actually knew about each other. Her earlier optimism faded, the needle swinging back toward dread. What if the more they learned about the other, the more they would come to despise each other?

She couldn't see that happening at the moment, but with the divorce rate in today's world...

They weren't getting married. So that was one thing they didn't have to worry about. And if they hated each other? Well, they could simply do a type of shared custody where Kaleb picked up their child every other weekend. If worse came to worst, they could do the exchange at a neutral location.

And if one of them moved out of state?

Ugh. Too much thinking! She needed to focus on the here and now and leave those kinds of worry for another day.

She took a sip of her tea, letting the cold, sweet liquid roll around on her tongue. She wasn't exactly sure what they were here to discuss other than the case. She was only eight weeks along. There was still a long time before the baby was born. But Kaleb had been in a hurry this morning and had seemed insistent. He hadn't changed his mind when she'd been examining Trey.

She pulled out her sketchbook. "So I've been going over the stuff about the baby."

"Baby? As in Trey or…"

"Trey, of course." She set her tea on the bench next to her and flipped open her book, placing it at an angle across her lap so that he could see. "So I compiled everything we know and everything I asked the Taylors about." She followed the path of the lines down several rows of boxes. "They came to the same conclusion you and his pediatrician did. Unless there's something that's not presenting any symptoms, it looks like Trey's diagnosis is right on target."

Kaleb took a huge sip of his lemonade before making a face.

"What's wrong? You don't agree?"

His throat moved as he swallowed, a bitter look on his face. "I agree that this lemonade doesn't have any sugar. No wonder he offered me packets of sweetener."

She laughed. "I thought you'd suddenly decided the case wasn't as simple after all."

"No. That case is simple." He put his own lemonade on the seat. "And unfortunately I'm stuck with surgical suite three."

"The one without the observation deck?"

"That's the one." His mouth was still making these funny-looking movements, as if trying to rid itself of the sour taste.

"Here, take a drink of mine." She held out her cup.

He glanced at her. "Are you sure?"

"Yes. I think we've already shared any germs we have." Her face heated as soon as the words were out of her mouth.

One side of his mouth went up. "Yes, I

guess we have. And they were definitely a whole lot sweeter than that lemonade."

The low tones slid over her, making her belly shimmy with need. A need that was going to have to sit there unattended. She was not going down that road again.

He took the glass and swallowed some of the liquid. "You definitely made the right choice as far as that goes."

Did that mean she hadn't made the right choice as far as keeping the baby? No, if that was the case he wouldn't want to be part of the child's life, would he? She decided to skip that topic for now.

"So if you're in surgical suite three, what does that mean? Can I still come in and observe as long as I stay out of the way?"

"Yes. I just wasn't sure if you would want to."

She blinked. "Why not?" Now that she'd seen baby Trey, she found she wanted to see his case to the end. Maybe it was the look in his parents' eyes when they looked at each other, the love so obvious that it hurt.

What would it be like to have that? She and Bill had been friends, but what she'd thought was love had turned out to be simple affection. The inferno that raged between her and Kaleb made what she'd had with Bill look like soggy embers. Warm, but with little fuel to keep it going.

At first she thought Kaleb wasn't going to answer her question, but then he said, "It was hard to hold that baby and not think about…"

She got it. Because she'd had the exact same feeling. "And not think about ours?"

"Yes."

"I know. I felt it, too. Especially when I held him. It was hard to hand him back."

"Yes, it was. Which brings us back to the reason why we're here." He settled back, stretching his legs out in front of them and crossing them at the ankles. "I wanted to go through a few things."

The man was tall. Really tall. She was five foot six and wasn't used to only coming up to a man's shoulders. But she did. And when he'd stretched out on the bed, she felt enveloped by him. The memory sent a shiver over her. Would their baby be tall? Would he or she have their daddy's looks?

She hoped so.

"Okay. Go ahead. I'm listening."

"I'd like to go to your prenatal appointments. Be there for the birth."

"What?" Shock speared through her, making her grab a couple of quick breaths. Any thoughts of her somehow doing her own thing until after the baby was born went out the window.

He frowned, turning to look at her. "Is that a problem? I'm letting you into my surgical suite."

"That's hardly the same thing." The thought of him being there when the doctor did intimate exams made her squirm. But why? What they'd done in his office had been about as personal as things got.

Maybe it was because this was in the cold light of day and the time in his office, she'd been…drunk. Again. Not with alcohol, but drunk with wanting him. Needing him.

Parts of her twitched to life, and she hurriedly moved her thoughts to less dangerous territory. "I guess I hadn't really thought about it. Is there a particular reason why you'd want to be there?"

"If I'm going to be a part of this baby's life—and I intend to, don't get me wrong— the earlier I can see the reality of what's happening and bond with him or her, the better, don't you agree?"

How could she not agree when he put it that way?

"B-but what about your job?"

"I'll do the same as you will, rearrange my schedule to fit in with those appointments."

"Are you sure, Kaleb? We could keep this a secret from people at the hospital. Keep this part of our lives private. My doctor will be at Grace Central."

"You've already chosen a doctor?"

"Yes, my ex, Bill, is an ob-gyn over there, and he—"

He stiffened beside her. "A man you were involved with is going to deliver our baby?"

She wasn't sure why he was getting upset. "Bill and I are still good friends. But, no, he's not delivering the baby. He did the initial pregnancy test and then referred me to another doctor." She smiled. "Who happens to be a woman, although that doesn't matter."

He was still frowning and a small thread of tension went through her. "Listen, this baby may be yours, but access to my private life is not. I'll do what I want, with whom I want."

After she said it, she realized how it

sounded, but there was no way to take back the words. And she wouldn't even if she could.

"I think you've made that perfectly clear."

The chill in his voice made her cringe. "I won't do anything to harm the baby. I need you to know that. But we're not a couple, Kaleb. You don't have the right to try to direct my life."

He muttered something under his breath that she didn't catch. She was beginning to feel like this was a mistake. Maybe she should walk back a couple of steps and tell him he wasn't welcome in the exam room with her. But that didn't seem fair. Or maybe it did. She wasn't sure of anything right now. On some plane, she'd realized this was going to be complicated, but she hadn't realized how complicated until this very moment.

She kept her voice as calm as she could. "Do we need to lay down some ground rules?"

"I don't know about that, but…"

Just then a teenager on a hoverboard glided by, his phone to his ear as he argued with someone. A girlfriend, judging from the heated tones. Nicola spied the bicycle from earlier coming back down the trail in the opposite direction. He, too, was on a phone. Except he wasn't talking. He was looking down at his screen driving with one hand.

"Kaleb!" She stood in a hurry.

He realized, too, and just as he opened his mouth to yell at them, the kid on the hoverboard saw the bike and used his weight to swerve out of the way. It worked, except he'd overcorrected, and before anyone could do anything, his board turned and plowed right into a nearby tree, knocking him backward onto the concrete. His head hit the hard surface with a dull thud. And then he was still.

Too still.

CHAPTER SEVEN

KALEB AND NICOLA jumped up from their bench, drinks and conversation forgotten as they rushed to the teen's aid. The bicyclist had already driven by, oblivious to what both of their distractions had caused.

Nicola dialed 911, while Kaleb kneeled down beside the downed kid. The operator answered, and she quickly relayed what they knew, telling her there were two doctors on the scene of a suspected head injury, and that they needed an ambulance.

"I'm going to put you on speaker, while I help." Nicola set down the phone and took vitals of the unconscious kid. He was breathing, at least. She glanced at his pupils. One was blown. Not good. "Kaleb, look."

He glanced over and swore softly.

The emergency services operator said,

"Central Park's medical unit is en route. They're about five minutes out."

"Okay, thanks." She gave the dispatcher the boy's vitals so she could pass them on. "His right pupil is blown. And there's a small amount of blood coming from the ear on that side."

Possible skull fracture. Her argument with Kaleb seemed so ridiculous now. Of course, he could come to her appointments. Could be a part of his child's life. Unlike her brother, who would never be anything more than a few stories told around the dinner table. The ache in her heart almost floored her, almost made her miss the dispatcher's next words.

"Can you secure his head and neck?"

"He's unconscious, so we can keep him still for as long as possible, but neither of us has any medical gear with us."

Nicola got up to direct another cyclist to the other side of the road. "Can you go down a ways and warn people that we've got a medical situation here and ask them to use a different route?"

"Sure. Is he going to be okay?" The woman's eyes were large. "He looks so young."

That had been Nicola's thought, as well. "We hope so. Thanks for your help."

She might not have been able to help her brother, but she could do something to help this boy. That's why she'd gone into medicine. To save lives.

The woman pedaled about fifty yards down the path and stopped, parking her bike sideways to make it more difficult for anyone just to zoom by her.

In the distance, Nicola thought she heard the sound of sirens, but she couldn't be sure. Just then, the boy moaned, his eyes fluttering. Kaleb put his hands on the boy's face. "You need to lie very still, okay?"

"My…head…" The words were slurred, trailing off at the end.

"I know it hurts. You've had an accident. Help is on its way, but for now we need you to lie here and rest, can you do that?"

"Think so."

The ambulance arrived on the scene, the vehicle emblazoned with the words Central Park Medical Unit. Two emergency services workers got out, one pulling a gurney from the back of the vehicle. It didn't take long for them to do their own assessment and get a neck brace and backboard in place.

"Thanks, you guys. We'll take it from here."

"Where are you taking him?"

"NYC Memorial," said one of the EMTs. Five minutes later, the patient was loaded up and headed back to Kaleb and Nicola's own hospital.

Nicola called ahead to let them know a trauma case was one the way. She waved at the bicyclist down the path, thanking her and letting her know she was free to go.

Kaleb took her arm. "You okay?"

"Yes, why wouldn't I be?" She paused, wondering if he was saying what she thought he was. "I'm going to work, Kaleb. For as long as I can. I love my job and don't plan to give it up, even after the baby's born."

"I know. I wouldn't expect anything different. But that doesn't mean I won't worry about the stress of what we do and how it might affect you and the baby."

She should be really irritated with him, but instead, she found his words touched her. Even if the concern wasn't for her so much as it was for the baby—at least it showed her that he would be a caring father.

So maybe they wouldn't end up hating each other after all. Maybe she'd find he had some really good character traits. Character traits that might make her start to…

A quick thought flitted through her head, and she dismissed it immediately. They'd both been working under the influence of adrenaline for the last bit of time. Coming down from it meant her thoughts were suspect right now. So were his. So she needed to extinguish any ideas that weren't based on reason.

Sitting back on the bench and taking a long drink of her sweet tea, she let the sugar course through her, hoping for a jolt of energy. "Well, I think I've had my excitement for the day."

"Yes. Me, too."

Ha! Well, Kaleb had had even more to deal with today than she had. She'd had a couple of days to get used to the idea of being pregnant. He hadn't. He'd had a matter of hours. Hours that he'd spent working cases like Trey's.

"So as to the question of my appointments, if you really want to come to them, I won't stop you. But please don't feel like I expect it." She paused. "I really don't expect anything out of you, Kaleb. My only reason for telling you was that I felt I owed it to you. Plus the fact that you were probably going to figure it out, once I started showing, anyway."

Something like a snort came from beside her. "Well, I appreciate you not making me find out that way."

"It wouldn't have been right. No matter how tempting that might have looked yesterday."

"So you thought about keeping me in the dark. It was the fear of getting caught that made you do the right thing?" There was a tightness to his voice that she didn't like.

"I hope not. But I have to be honest and say it went through my head before I finally decided to tell you." She licked her lips. "Saying that, I'd really rather not tell anyone at the hospital. Not for a while. Maybe not at all. If my appointments are at Grace Central that might make it a little easier to contain."

"Any particular reason you want it kept a secret?"

Her eyebrows shot up. "You *want* people to know?"

He stared off into the distance. "I hadn't given it a lot of thought. But I do have a friend who is bound to figure it out. I'd like to tell him at some point. Just to make it easier on me. Not that that will be a fun conversation."

"I understand. And I'll tell my parents, of course. They'll probably want to meet you." She couldn't imagine a more awkward scenario than sitting there while her dad grilled Kaleb on whatever questions came to mind. But if Kaleb truly wanted to be a part of this baby's life, he was going to meet them at some point. Better to do that sooner rather than later.

"That's fine. So when is your first appointment?"

"In about a week. I'm thirty-five, so they're going to want to monitor me a bit more closely than their younger patients."

He smiled. "You say that like you're ancient, Nicola. I'm thirty-eight."

"Wow, you really are an old man, aren't you?"

When his lips curved, bringing that deadly craggy line in his cheek into play, she gulped and quickly added, "Speaking of ages. Anything on your side of the family I should know about? Genetic conditions?"

His smile turned sober. "No. Not that I'm aware of."

"Okay, nothing on mine, either, except a general absence of luck, I guess. When you said something about a double layer of protection that day in your office, it almost made me laugh. I'd thought if only we'd pulled out two packets instead of just one, this might not have happened."

"Remind me to never use you as a good-luck charm then, while gambling."

For some reason, that stung and she wasn't quite sure why. As if realizing it, he put a hand on hers. "I was joking. It was a simple defect in the condom or packaging. It had nothing to do with luck, bad or otherwise."

"Sorry. I know I'm on edge right now. I'm hoping my hormones don't suddenly decide they're not going to play nicely anymore. I'll do my best not to boo-hoo on your best shirt or anything."

Except she'd already done that. When she'd talked to him about her brother's death. But that hadn't been because of hormones. That had been because there'd been an actual tragedy in her family. A tragedy that was still taking its toll on her and her parents.

She sucked down a deep breath "Okay, so anything else we need to go over?"

"I can't think of anything. Let me know how things go with your parents when you decide to tell them. I'll have to tell my mom and dad, as well. And, like I said, I'll need to tell Snow."

Snow. The man she'd met at the restaurant. The one who'd given her a funny look. "Sounds good. I want to wait a couple of weeks until after my first exam before saying anything to them. Just in case something goes wrong."

Just saying those words made her heart cramp. What if they found something that shouldn't be there. What if her pregnancy hormones really were due to something awful, like a molar pregnancy.

No. She was pregnant. Something inside of her had whispered in her ear even before she'd taken the home pregnancy test. She'd known.

And now, so did Kaleb. The hard part was over. At least she hoped it was. Because if it wasn't, then with the exception of her brother's death, these might be the hardest nine months she'd ever have to endure. As she watched Kaleb pick up their trash and take it to the nearest waste receptacle, she sucked down a deep breath. She needed to be on her guard. Because those pregnancy hormones might not simply cause weepy moments here and there. What if they deceived her and made her think she had feelings for Kaleb? Like she'd had when she'd thought of his character traits?

Any feelings like that would be traitorous, and likely to disappear as soon as the baby was born.

Oh, Lord, had that already happened? What if that incident in his office had been dictated by the baby chemicals that were coursing through her veins? If that was the case, she'd have to be more careful from now on. Any mushy feelings she might develop for Kaleb she was going to attribute to hormones, plain and simple. She'd just have to wait it out and ignore them as much as she could. Then once the baby was born, she could sort out what was and what wasn't real. She held on to that thought as they walked out of the park and each got in their separate cars, and continued to hold it as she took the exit that led to home. And it remained on her mind as she drifted off to sleep later that night.

Saturday found Kaleb in surgical room three waiting for Nicola to get gloved up and in the room. Her last case had run over by fifteen minutes and she said she was on her way. He had a schedule to keep, but he didn't want to start this without her, and he wasn't sure why.

He hadn't seen her all day on Friday, but that was probably just as well. He wasn't quite sure why he'd insisted on being there other than it seemed strange to just ignore the baby until after it was born and then suddenly start making appearances in the child's life. What if Nicola decided during that time that she wanted to do this on her own?

Not happening. So it was better to be there than to sit on the bench and pretend he didn't want to be in the game.

The door to the room opened and Nicola entered with her hands held out for her gloves. She wasn't taking an active part in the surgery and now that she was here, his nerves were acting up.

"Okay, we're ready to start." He glanced

at the anesthesiologist, who nodded and adjusted his instruments to deepen sedation.

"Go ahead."

His eyes found Nicola's, before his glance dropped to her stomach. How would he feel if this was his child and Nicola was watching him work?

Ridiculous. There is no way he could work on his child or any other relative.

Choosing his first tool, he studied the baby's lip. He would make the repair using the rotation-and-advancement method, where the side of the defect nearest the nostril would be rotated down to join the lips together and the other side would be "advanced" to fill the hole created by the rotation.

Clearing his throat, he began to talk his way through the procedure to document each step. Out of the corner of his eye, he saw Nicola take a step closer so she could see.

"Could someone turn the screen on?"

Someone flipped a button and the screen on the wall across from him flickered to life. It wasn't just for the diagnostician's benefit. It was also to help the entire team see exactly what Kaleb was seeing through the little camera mounted on the side of his lighted loupes.

"Making the rotation incision. Scalpel, please."

He held his hand out and the surgical nurse placed the tool on his palm.

The first cut is always deep.

The words to a familiar song whispered through his head. It wasn't just the deepest. It also had to be the most accurate for Trey to have a natural appearance.

He gauged the space he needed to cover with the flap. Normally, Kaleb was only minimally aware of the rest of his team in the room. He got into a zone where no one existed except for him and his patient. Only this time, there was a third person in his little circle. Nicola.

He could feel her gaze on him, feel the tension crackling off of her in waves as she followed his progress. If it had been him watching, his hand would be curling around an imaginary scalpel, planning how he would make the incisions. Where he would place each suture. But those were things he couldn't think about right now.

"Rotating the flap and moving it into place. Could someone adjust my loupes a bit to my right, please?"

Hands moved in to do his bidding, then backed away to get a fresh pair of surgical gloves. They had to make sure the surgical field was as free from contamination as possible. This child would not get another chance at this if infection ate away the repair.

With the loupes adjusted, he could see without having to compensate and he moved the flap down to where he'd prepared one side of the lips. It was just a bit tight. So he modified the incision he'd made to help ease the tension.

He secured the innermost part of the repair with dissolving sutures, continuing to describe what he was doing, both for the surgical record and for Nicola's benefit. She'd said she had never seen a cleft repaired before. But that wasn't the only reason she wanted to be here. They'd both talked about how moved they'd been by this child and how it was probably due to the fact that their own child was growing in Nicola's womb at this very second.

Right now, he was glad his expressions were hidden by both the mask and the loupes, because he wouldn't want Nicola to see his eyes. His tension was probably tighter right now than that flap's had been. Only unlike what he'd done with his scalpel, there was no easing this particular tension.

When he got to the outermost part of the repair, he made his stitches as tiny as he could without compromising the strength of the sutures. He adjusted the fit so that the Cupid's bow on the repair side matched that of the other side.

That was about as good as it was going to get. "Rotation completed. Starting the advancement procedure."

He eyed his incision site, using the measurements he'd taken during the baby's exam. His notes were displayed on the screen along with his camera's view. He moved his scalpel a little more to the right.

This should be like second nature to him by now. He'd done a number of these repairs, including volunteering with a medical unit overseas to help impoverished areas. Those children were all equally important, but somehow his performance right now wasn't by rote. He was considering each and every move he made.

Maybe he needed to be doing that with Nicola. Not just coasting along and hoping for the best, but considering every move and its ramifications.

A sound caught his ear. A little blip that stood out from the rest of the background noise. The steady rhythm that always accompanied his surgeries. When they were going well. He ignored it. His scalpel hovered over the incision site just as it came again. A syncopated sound that made him look up and lock eyes with his anesthesiologist. "What's going on, John?"

"Not sure. He's just thrown a couple of PVCs. I'll let you know if they become concerning."

PVCs weren't uncommon during surgery, and normally he just took them in stride unless they became frequent. But right now, his ears were super tuned to the sound. He waited a beat or two and then forced his muscles to relax, wondering if Nicola were as tense as he was at this moment.

"Making the incision."

His scalpel sliced true, freeing the skin to move forward. As if fitting a piece to a jigsaw puzzle, the flap filled the hole perfectly, just as another off-rhythm blip hit his ears.

Every muscle in his gut tightened. "Do I need to stop?"

"No. We're still okay."

Forcing himself to ignore the monitor, he sutured the flap in place, his hand surprisingly steady as he molded the baby's new lip.

When the last suture was in place, he looked at the repair with critical eyes, searching for any puckers in the baby's skin that would cause problems later. But the little zig-zag-looking line was smooth and even, and the bows on the baby's lips looked symmetrical.

Another blip. A double this time.

Hell. He needed to call it before this turned into something worse. "Okay, the last suture is in place."

He dropped the instrument into the stainless steel bowl on the table and glanced at his anesthesiologist. The man looked totally unconcerned. As well he should. Kaleb was the one who was having a fit over it.

"Easing back on the sedation."

The cramped muscles in his stomach were starting to ease as he took in the cardiac monitor that was now beeping with nice steady points of sound. Nothing bad had happened, except in his mind.

What if their child had an emergency? Had to have surgery? Was he going to turn into a basket case while in the waiting room, imagining every possible thing that could go wrong?

Judging from his emotions right now? Probably.

He glanced over at Nicola and saw her eyes were glassy as if she, too, had been riding the same emotional roller coaster as he had.

But now it was over and he could get off the ride. He looked around. "Good work, people. We just helped a little boy lead a more normal life."

The atmosphere in the room turned gleeful as people clapped and congratulated him. He didn't want it, any of it. He had just wanted to do his best for this boy.

He went over to John Laroby and nodded. "Thanks. Sorry for pointing out the PVCs."

In reality, John was one of the best anesthesiologists the hospital had. If anyone was aware of the tiniest nuances of sedation it was him.

"I understand. It's a baby. I always get keyed up when we work on them."

"Yeah. Me, too." Except he didn't. Not usually. And he wasn't sure he liked being this involved in one's care. It had to be due to finding out he was going to be a father.

Nicola made to leave the room and gave him a quick wave. He moved to join her, waiting as she discarded her mask and gloves, and then joined her once he'd gotten rid of his.

"How'd it look?"

She nodded with a tilt to her head. "I was impressed."

"Hey, I wasn't looking for accolades, just wanted to know if the repair looked okay."

"You know it does." She smiled. "I have to tell you, I was a nervous wreck, though. I don't know how you do it."

"I was a little nervous on this one, as well."

"Because of the baby?" she said, probably not realizing she'd hit the nail on the head.

"Yes. It was hard not to imagine how I'd feel if Trey were mine. I really wanted to do right by him."

"And you did. But I have to tell you, I'm glad it's over. Especially when you heard his cardiac sounds change. It was hard for me to just stand there."

"John's a great anesthesiologist. I'm sure he was on top of it."

"I'm sure. It doesn't change how I felt, though, when I heard them."

He leaned a shoulder against the wall, noting how tightly her hands were clasped. "Hey, he's fine. It worked out just the way it should have."

Sudden moisture appeared in her eyes. "I know. And I'm just being silly. It's hormones, I'm sure."

"It's the reaction of a human being that is hoping for a good outcome."

She touched his hand, her smile doing something to his insides. "And there was a good outcome, wasn't there? I'm so glad for Trey and his family."

"Me, too." He sucked down a deep breath and decided to tackle a question that had been at the back of his mind all day. "Do you have your appointment date yet?"

"Are you sure you want to come?"

"Absolutely." He was more sure now than he'd been when he'd started the surgery. He wasn't sure why, other than the fact that he needed to be there. No matter how hard it would be when she took the baby home and left him behind.

"It's on Friday."

"Okay. Do you want me to pick you up?"

She hesitated, moistening her lips. "Do you want to?"

"It might not be a bad idea, just in case we need to talk about something."

"Okay. That sounds like a plan." Her smile had faded and something he couldn't read replaced it. "Good job again. Thanks for letting me watch."

"You're welcome. I'll see you next week, then, if not sooner."

CHAPTER EIGHT

NICOLA'S APPOINTMENT WAS the same day the hoverboard accident victim was scheduled to be released from the hospital. Both Kaleb and the diagnostician had peeked in on the boy, since Nicola had been called on to assess some of the test findings. He'd had a skull fracture, like they suspected, but he'd been very lucky not to have any neck or back injuries to go along with that diagnosis. If bad things came in packages of three, he hoped that good things did, as well.

So all that was left on today's agenda was Nic's prenatal appointment. He'd taken the rest of the day off, just so he didn't have to hurry back if there were any problems.

Problems.

Like those blips on Trey's heart monitor during surgery? What if they found something when they did the ultrasound?

Strangely, Nicola was as calm as he was keyed up. Maybe it was an act. Kind of like the performance she'd given when she pretended not to know who he was, when she first came to the hospital. That seemed so long ago now. So much had happened since then.

Actually it had happened even before that first meeting at the hospital. The gears had already been set into motion. Except neither of them had realized it at the time.

He was going to be a father. Heaven help them all. His lips curved in a smile. And he and Nicola had actually come to some kind of a truce, or an unspoken understanding or something, because things were going fairly smoothly. Maybe a little too smoothly.

Would he meet her ex while he was there? He wasn't sure why, but it bothered him that a past romantic interest was involved in any way, shape or form with the birth of his child. It was ridiculous. If Kaleb's ex showed up on the scene, he would be surprised if Nicola gave her a second look. And maybe that bothered him, as well.

His suspicions that she'd slept with him the second time as a way to tell him about the pregnancy had begun fading away. And when he'd seen the emotion on her face while holding baby Trey, any remaining doubts had died completely. She'd had no way of knowing how he'd react to the news about the pregnancy. But she would have equally not known how he'd react after they'd finished making love.

Right?

Men were supposed to be more mellow after sex. But…

No, don't go there again. It won't help anything. Now if she makes a habit out of sleeping with you and then bringing up difficult subjects afterward, then you might have reason to be suspicious.

Not that they were going to sleep together again.

He was on his guard. And he suspected she was, too, if the way they avoided touching the other was anything to go by.

He'd had to cancel his plans to have drinks with Snow—again—but he promised they'd get together sometime next week.

His phone buzzed and he glanced at the readout, frowning. It was Nicola. Hopefully she wasn't going to change her mind about him coming to the appointment. "Hello?"

"Hi, um, it's me, Nicola."

"I know who it is." He smiled. Being pregnant hadn't softened her crisp matter-of-fact tones. So far, the only thing that had had the power to do that had been…

Sex.

"Oh. Well, um, Cade is asking to see you to say goodbye. So are his parents."

It took him a moment to filter through who Cade was and then realized it was the hoverboard victim. "What time?"

"Well…now. I told you about it yesterday."

She had? Oh, hell, she had. They'd passed in the hallway and she'd asked if he was coming. But he hadn't written it down. "Okay, tell them I'll be there in just a few minutes."

"Sounds good."

They were supposed to go to her appointment in about a half hour, so hopefully Cade's discharge wouldn't take too long. He somehow doubted she'd want to skate out early.

It didn't take him long to get to the pediatric ward on the second floor. Decorated in bright colors with pictures mixed in with paintings of animals in humorous poses and clothing, this ward was the only part of the hospital that had large blocks of color in the linoleum flooring. Everything about it spelled fun and health, a subliminal message to heal and get better. He stopped by the nurses station. "Hoverboard accident victim?" Sometimes it was easier to go by a patient's condition than try to remember all their names.

"Room two-oh-one. They're waiting for you, Dr. Sabat."

"Thanks." He headed down the hallway, hearing laughter coming from the distance. One of those voices belonged to Nicola. How he knew that he wasn't sure. But somewhere along the way, his brain had learned to recognize her throaty tones. His brain immediately retrieved a facial expression to go along with that laugh. When had he memorized that? He wasn't sure, but he had. It was a smile that made tiny crinkles stand out on either side of her nose...making her eyes light up.

Not something he should be focusing on right now. He was here to keep a promise to a patient. Nothing more, nothing less.

He gave a quick knock on the door and then walked in. Cade was sitting on the side of his bed, struggling to put on his socks. A woman hovered nearby, concern clearly chiseled on her face.

"Are you sure I shouldn't—?"

"Mom, I can do it. Just give me a minute or two."

He wasn't sure what they'd been laughing at a second ago, but Nicola's face didn't have a trace of the smile he'd just drawn up from memory.

He turned his attention to the patient. "How are you doing?"

Cade looked up. "Dr. Sabat, you came! Nicola wasn't sure you'd be able to. She said you might have an emergency."

So she'd covered for him. Because he'd forgotten something important.

His jaw tightened. And once he had a child, was he going to forget important events in its life, too? Would Nic have to cover for him? Make up excuses for why he didn't show up for a ballet recital? Or a high-school graduation? Or the birth of a child?

The reality of what was coming suddenly made itself known to him. He would need to reset some of his priorities.

He glanced at Nic, who still wasn't smiling. Was she thinking the same thing he was? That she might need to prod his memory at every turn? Send him text messages, then have to apologize for nagging him? It wouldn't be nagging. And he was going to make it a point not to forget.

"Sorry I'm late." He smiled at Cade. It was funny how the boy called Nic by her given name and yet used Kaleb's title. Maybe there was more softness to her than he gave her credit for. Or maybe she just showed it to people other than him.

That made him wince. Did he bring out a side of her that other people didn't see?

"My dad says I need to lay off the hoverboard for a while."

"That's probably not a bad idea, until your balance is back up to where it should be." Hopefully the kid had learned his lesson about talking on the phone while trying to guide it. The same with the bicyclist who'd been texting at the time, although Kaleb doubted that person had even been aware of what had transpired. Hopefully he saw it in the news and realized...and changed his priorities.

Just like Kaleb needed to do.

"I was on the phone when it happened, you know." Cade said it with a touch of shame in his voice.

"I know. It's a good lesson, don't you think? You were very lucky you weren't injured worse than you were." Kaleb left out the fact that the boy could have died. But somehow he bet Cade was well aware of how lucky he'd been. Or maybe his parents had laid down the law. Maybe that was part of the reason the hoverboard was on hiatus.

"I promised my mom and dad that I'd never do that again. And when I start driving I won't do it, either. I'd heard about what could happen, but I never really thought it would. I know better now."

"I'm glad, Cade."

Just then a nurse came in with some papers. "Are you ready to get out of this place?"

"Am I ever."

Cade's parents came over to Kaleb. "Nicola told us what you did. We are so grateful."

"She had just as much to do with it as I did. I'm just glad we were there, and that he's going to be okay. There's a bicyclist who was just as much at fault as Cade was."

"Yes, Nicola told us. Thank you again for everything."

Well, it seemed like Nicola had everything under control. As usual. He was beginning to think Grace Central had lost more than they realized. Hopefully they didn't suddenly look around and decide to woo her back. Because if that happened, he might just need to…

To what? Do some wooing of her himself?

Uh, no. There would be no wooing or anything else. He was done with that. Once and for all. Wasn't he?

Cade's parents signed the papers and with their son in a wheelchair, they were seen out and into the car.

Nicola came over and bumped his shoulder with hers. "Well, that was certainly a happy ending, wasn't it? I honestly didn't think he was going to be that lucky."

"Nor did I." He glanced at her jeans and thin T-shirt, and realized she'd already changed in preparation of going to her appointment. "You look like you're ready."

"I am…but…"

His chest tightened. Was she having second thoughts about him going with her? "But?"

"If you don't want to come, please don't feel like—"

"I want to. I haven't changed my mind."

She nodded. "Okay, then, if you're sure. I can't wait for you to see my… I mean, the hospital I used to work at."

He blinked. Maybe it wouldn't be Grace Central that would come looking to win Nicola back. Maybe it would be Nicola who would decide that NYC Memorial was not what she'd been looking for and would decide to head home to New Jersey.

And if that happened?

Well, if it did, he'd let her go and do his best not to watch her as she walked away, taking their baby with her.

CHAPTER NINE

NICOLA WAS LYING on the cold table, her nerves in knots, clammy hands clasped together on her stomach. Why had she let Kaleb come in the room with her? Or thought it a good idea for him to come with her at all?

She'd needed moral support, that's why.

The door opened, and Bill came in, letting it swing closed behind him. "Dr. Banks has been called to do an emergency C-section. So sorry, Nic. You're stuck with me. This time, anyway."

"It's okay." She swiveled her head to look at Kaleb. "This is Dr. Sabat—Kaleb. He's…a friend. He agreed to come with me."

"That was nice of you, Kaleb. Nic could use a friend right now, I'm sure. I'm Bill. I'm one of her friends, too. From a ways back."

"Sorry," she said. "I should have introduced you, too."

A frown came over Kaleb's face. Had he not wanted her to tell Bill his name? Well, what was she supposed to do? Just pretend he didn't exist?

Like that first night they were together?

Looking back, it seemed kind of silly. But she'd been mortified over what had happened—had been afraid that he'd judge her for having a one-night stand.

But what about him? She could have just as easily judged him for sleeping with her.

Bill glanced at the chart. "So it looks like you're starting week nine. We should be able to get a look at that heartbeat today on the ultrasound."

Nicola hadn't even thought about that. She'd be able to see her baby's heart?

Kaleb cleared his throat. "You're going to do the exam, then?"

"Yep. Just the ultrasound part, though. Don't worry." He smiled at Nic. "I take it he knows about us."

"He does. But it doesn't matter. I just want to make sure everything is okay with the baby."

Bill nodded. "Well, then, let's get started."

Nicola unzipped her jeans and parted them,

then glanced at Kaleb and was surprised to see his face had taken on a dull red hue that she'd never seen before. At least not on him. Surely he wasn't embarrassed. Not after what they'd done together.

She didn't have much time to think about it as icy lubricant plopped onto the bare skin of her belly. "Yikes, could that be any colder?"

Bill laughed. "Sorry about that."

Dipping the wand of the ultrasound machine in the stuff, he drew the instrument over her stomach. The machine came to life in a series of dark-and-light images that she couldn't make heads or tails of. She thought 3D was supposed to be clearer than the older versions.

"Okay, here we go, so pay attention, Nic."

She stared at the screen, not sure what she was looking at. Then she saw it. A tiny C-shaped object. She could make out a head, a chest…

"There it is. We have a beating heart."

She caught sight of a flickering on the screen and realized that was it. Her baby's heart was pulsing inside of her. "Oh, God."

All of a sudden the cold table and the even colder lubricant were forgotten.

This was real. Very real. Her baby's image was on that screen.

Up until now, the readings on those pregnancy sticks had been some abstract thing that she knew existed, but couldn't see. That couldn't affect her, except for the brief bouts of nausea she'd experienced. But to *see* it. To see that steady flickering light in the object's chest.

"Kaleb..."

"I know. I see it." Something in his voice dragged her attention from the screen, and she caught him leaning forward in his chair, his gaze intent on what was happening on the screen in front of them. It reminded her of how he'd been as he'd operated on baby Trey.

He was invested. Truly invested in this child's life. She wasn't sure it would be as real for him as it was for her when the time came. But it definitely was.

A lump formed in her throat, and she turned her attention back to the monitor. "Is the baby's heart rate normal?"

"A little quick, but stress can do that. Probably feeding off some of his or her mama's energy."

Energy was right. Her nerves were jumping here and there and there was no way she could calm them. Nor did she want to. She wanted to savor this moment, to commit it to memory forever.

Kaleb's voice came through. "How much is 'a little quick'?"

"Only about five beats a minute faster than the norm. It's perfectly okay. If I didn't know better, I'd say you're as nervous as a new fath…" Bill's voice trailed off, and he looked at her, asking a question with his eyes.

He knew. He'd always been intuitive. She gave him a nod.

"Wow, congratulations, then. To both of you." Bill did something with the screen and then pushed some buttons. A paper slid from a slot on the side of the machine. "Just a little something to take home with you. Do you have a name picked out yet?"

"No. I… We haven't even talked about that part yet."

"Well, there's still plenty of time for that," he said.

Kaleb had been oddly silent. "Are you okay?" she asked.

"Just not what I expected to see."

What wasn't? A baby? *His* baby?

She wanted to take his hand and squeeze it. To feel his fingers in hers letting her know everything was going to be okay, but that wasn't appropriate. They weren't a couple, despite what Bill might be thinking. They were just two people who happened to have exchanged some DNA and mixed up a child in the process.

Bill nodded. "It can be overwhelming the first time."

Said as if she and Kaleb were going to have other times. Other babies. But they weren't. This was it. The only baby the two of them would ever make together. And that gave her a funny, queasy sensation that was very different from her light bouts of morning sickness. This had a more permanent feel to it. There was a finality that didn't go down as easy as it should.

After retrieving the piece of paper from the ultrasound machine, Bill handed it to her. She stared at the first picture of her baby and took in the tiny precious features. And, yes, they were precious. Already. "So he or she does look okay, right?"

"Yes, like I said, so far, so good. We'll keep an eye on that heart rate, just in case, but I suspect it's just a one-off thing. Just take care of yourself. Don't overdo the caffeine and no alcohol. But then you know all of this."

"I do, but thanks. When do I need to come back?"

"Let's see you in a couple of weeks. Hopefully you'll be able to meet Dr. Banks next time."

Kaleb had gone quiet. Lord, she hoped he wasn't regretting coming, or worse, everything that went along with it. Well, if he was, she would make it clear that he could back out at any time. At least up until the baby was born. If he didn't want to do this, he needed to speak up. And soon. Because the last thing she wanted was for her baby to have a dad for three or four years and then have him disappear once he found someone he loved and they started a family of their own.

She swallowed as a shot of reality made its way through her system.

She hadn't thought about what would happen if Kaleb fell in love with someone. But maybe she should. Because the odds were very good that he would, eventually. Kaleb was a gorgeous man that any woman in her right mind would be lucky to have.

Well, any woman except for her. She wasn't in the market for a man, whether it was Kaleb or someone else. She had too much on her plate right now.

They said their goodbyes and made their way out to Kaleb's car. Once he got in, she turned to him. "What's wrong?"

"Nothing."

"Don't give me that, Kaleb. If you want to opt out, just say so, and it will be fine."

He stared out of the windshield for a moment before glancing over at her. "Is my being here with you upsetting you?"

"Upsetting me? What do you mean?"

"The baby's heart rate. Bill said it's higher than it should be, and it made me wonder if it's because I was there with you. He talked about stress and—"

"No. It's not that." She stopped to think about how to put it. His presence had made her nervous, but not in a bad way. It was more of a feeling of guilt for him having to come at all. "Bill also said it was probably nothing. I *was* nervous. I admit it. But more because this was my first appointment, and I was afraid maybe something would be wrong with the baby. What if my brother's illness is somehow bound up in this baby's genetic code? So, yes, there were plenty of things for me to be nervous about. But your being here is not one of them. At least not in the way you're thinking. I just don't want you to feel trapped."

He reached over and gripped her hand for a long second, the way she'd wanted him to in the exam room. "I don't feel trapped. I feel… a sense of awe. I can't believe that baby is something we did together. I mean, what we did was great—more than great, don't get me wrong—but I never dreamed it would result in… A baby. A tiny human being."

"I know. I felt the same way."

"I want to be at your next appointment. And all the rest of them."

She smiled. "Thank you. It helps me to feel like I'm not so alone in all of this."

"You're not alone. And you won't be through any of this."

For the first time since her brother's death, she actually believed those words—believed that maybe this time she wouldn't have to be the one who left.

"My parents want to meet you." The words were said hesitantly, softly, as if they'd been dragged from her.

They were standing outside of the hospital entrance, off to the side, speaking in hushed tones.

"I thought you were going to wait a couple of weeks to tell them."

"I was. But then my mom saw Bill in the grocery store, and he congratulated her on becoming a grandma, without realizing she didn't know. He clammed up immediately when she questioned him on it, but it was too late. The damage was done. So then, I had to field a call—on speakerphone, of all things—from my mom and dad demanding to know why they had to hear about the baby from Bill. Why hadn't I at least called them to tell them personally." She rolled her eyes. "This was so not the way I wanted this to happen."

He could imagine. Because it wasn't the way he'd imagine this would go, either. He hadn't expected them to want to meet him. But, honestly, his parents were going to do the same as soon as they found out. And how could they not? They were going to want to be involved in the baby's life, just like he did. How much easier would it have been if they were a couple?

But they weren't, and pretending to be just for their parents' sake was far beyond the scope of what he was willing to do. Because it would come crashing down around his ears. There was no way around that.

Best just to make the introductions and then just keep things low-key after that. Nicola wouldn't be with him on days he kept the baby. They could just do a pass-off at a supermarket or something. He'd put the baby in his vehicle on his days and hand him or her back when it was Nicola's turn.

And if that seemed complicated and a little cold-blooded, well…it was. But there was no way around it. And it was how it had to be if he wanted to be involved in his child's life.

"I can understand them wanting to meet me. Do they know the situation?"

"They know we're coworkers and that it just…happened. I didn't have the heart to tell my mom I'd gotten pregnant as the result of a one-night stand with a man I met at a bar. And that my grief over Danny precipitated it."

It would be pretty hard to face her dad and look him in the eye, if she had. Somehow that ideal no-commitment ritual he'd built in to his dating habits didn't look quite as appealing as it once had.

Don't spend the night? Ever? It actually

seemed pretty selfish looking back at it from where he now stood.

But to try to change now would be to risk falling into another relationship and trying to make it work. Something he wasn't quite willing to do. Not yet, at least.

"So other than surprise, how was their reaction to the news?" He could imagine his parents might be a little disappointed in him. And maybe he was a little disappointed in himself. But even Nicola had said she didn't want marriage. She'd said it before he even had a chance to bring it up.

"It was awkward. And I think they were in shock. But once that wears off, I hope they'll be happy for us. I mean as far as the baby goes."

"Any idea when they want this meeting to take place?"

She rolled her eyes. "They want me to invite you to dinner. Soon." She touched his sleeve. "I'll understand if you don't want to. My parents will just have to understand that while you want to be in their grandchild's life, you don't necessarily want to be in theirs."

He could understand their concern. This was their grandbaby. They felt protective and wanted to check out the baby's father for themselves. His parents were probably going to want to do the same with her, although he was definitely going to put that off for a while, if he could. Especially since he was still a little worried about stress hormones and Nicola's health, despite her reassurances.

By refusing to go to dinner, would he be opening her up to more stress? Or would he be relieving stress? Maybe that was the question to ask.

"Would my going make it easier or harder on you and your relationship with them?"

"Do you want my honest answer?"

"I really do."

She bit the corner of her lip. His insides immediately took notice. "I think it would relieve some of their worry that you're…say, a sex predator or something. I—" she smiled "—*vouched* for you, like you did for me once upon a time, but I think they want to see it with their own eyes."

It was pretty much what he'd thought. "Well, then I'll go to dinner. How hard could it be?"

"You haven't met my parents." She batted her eyes at him. "So now that we have that out of the way, what are you doing tonight? Inquiring moms want to know."

"Tonight? You said soon, but wow." He laughed. "She's not letting any grass grow under her feet—or mine—is she?"

"My mom is pretty much always ready for company. She keeps a freezer full of entrées that she's cooked ahead of time, so it's just a matter of pulling one out and whipping up a salad to go with it."

His eyebrows went up. "I think I see where you get your organizational skills."

"If you think I'm organized… My mom is over the top. But you'll like her. You'll like them both. They're not going to grill you or make snap judgments. They just want to meet you. No pressure, okay?"

"I'll take your word for it. So what time does she want us there? I'm off at six."

"I'm off early, so I can meet you at their house." She pulled a slip of paper from her purse and scribbled something on it. "This is their address. And, like I said, don't worry. It will be a snap."

It wasn't a snap. From the moment he put their address into his GPS and started heading for the Bradley household, his nerves were pretty much toast. She might think they'd be nonjudgmental, but when he looked at it from the standpoint of his own upbringing, he was pretty sure his parents would be asking him some hard questions. Not about the pregnancy, since those things happen, but over the fact that he'd slept with her with no intention of ever seeing her again.

Hadn't Nicola said she left out that part of her explanation to her parents. So it wasn't just his mom and dad who'd look askance at that. Of course, his parents had been disappointed over his two broken engagements, too. Especially since his sister was, by all accounts, very happy in her marriage. Her second child was due in about a month.

How did they do it? How did his parents, his sister, make that kind of commitment?

Maybe the same way he was making a commitment to be there for his child. No matter what happened. The thought rolled around in his head for a while looking for someplace to lodge.

He crossed the Jersey line at about six thirty. They didn't live very far from the place where Nicola and her brother used to work, so he had five or six more minutes before he arrived. Dinner was planned for six forty-five, so he should be right on time.

Grace Central was on his right-hand side. Was Nicola's ex working tonight? He wondered what her parents had thought of him. The man was like a saint compared to Kaleb.

And he really needed to stop thinking about this or he was going to take the next exit out of town.

Commitment, remember? It's not always going to be easy.

Another two minutes and he was on their street looking for the house number. He saw a brick two-story structure with two rocking chairs on the porch. Red pillows were propped perfectly on each one. He pulled into their driveway and turned off the car.

As soon as he did, the door burst open and a woman stood there, her dark red locks almost the exact same shade as Nicola's. Speaking of Nicola, he didn't see her car here. Hopefully she was inside.

He climbed out of his vehicle and started up the walk, carrying a box containing her parents' favorite wine, according to Nicola.

"Hello. You must be Kaleb. I'm Margaret. Dan is cooking steaks on the grill." She pulled him into a quick embrace, then let him go.

Dan. Nicola's brother must have been named after his father. That had to make things even harder. Something else she said caught at his attention. Didn't Nicola say her mom would just pull a premade meal out of the freezer and heat it up? "You didn't have to go to any trouble."

"No trouble, of course. And a good excuse for Dan to use his grill."

"I brought some wine."

"Why, thank you. Come on in."

She stepped aside to let him in to the house. Walking across the threshold, the scent of freshly baked bread tickled his nostrils. "Is Nicola here yet?"

"She's helping her dad, so yes. She's around back. Her car is parked in the garage."

That's why he hadn't seen it.

Following Margaret as she led the way through a living area that had an airy and open feel, he glanced around at the interior. Unlike Nicola, they evidently didn't have a problem with having their son's pictures displayed on the walls, since there were family portraits in several different places. Danny and Nicola looked a lot alike. If he didn't know better, he'd think they were twins. Continuing to follow Margaret's lead, they arrived in the kitchen. It was large and sprawling without losing that inviting feel that the rest of the house had. "It smells wonderful in here."

"Thank you." She glanced over at him. "So you work with Nicola?"

He hadn't expected the question, and it took him a minute to shift gears and think of a suitable reply. "We don't always work directly together, but we do work at the same hospital, yes." He decided to explain further, and added, "I've consulted with her on a case or two. She's very good at what she does."

"She is thorough. Always has been."

Margaret pulled the wine from the box and stooped to put it in a wine cooler under the cabinet. "Let's join the others outside."

Actually, Kaleb was glad to oblige, since if any questions got awkward, he'd have an excuse for sweating. When he went through the sliding glass door, however, he saw that her idea of outside and his were two different things. While they were technically out on a patio, they were under a covered pergola, where a lazy ceiling fan spun in circles. Sweeping layers of mosquito netting were artfully gathered around the supporting poles and tied with white ribbon. The grill was no metal prefab deal, either, but had been constructed from bricks that matched the ones on the house. It was vented through a chimney that went through the top of the pergola.

Nicola came over and nudged his arm. "Everything okay?"

"Yep, just fine."

"No trouble finding it?"

"Nope."

"Good."

The rapid questions made it hard to gauge her mood. But she didn't seem nervous or irritated.

She smiled at her mom. "It looks like you two introduced yourselves."

"We did," Margaret said. "Why don't you take Kaleb over to meet your dad, while I get the bread out of the oven."

"Okay."

He leaned closer to her ear. "I thought you said dinner would be something simple."

"I thought it would be. It's the way she normally does things. I guess they decided to go all out today. Sorry." She went around to the side of the grill. "Daddy, I want you to meet Kaleb Sabat. Kaleb, this is my father, Dan."

Dan laid his tongs across the grill's grate and reached out to shake his hand. "Nice to meet you, Kaleb. We're hearing a lot about you."

Was there a *finally* implied in that phrase?

"You as well, sir."

"You're just in time, because I think these are about done." He forked up thick steaks and laid them on a platter. "Not sure if you're a medium guy or a well-done guy, but medium will be on the left and well is on the right."

Right about now, Kaleb was feeling pretty well-done, and dinner—and the questions—hadn't even started yet.

Dan set the food on the table in the middle of the patio and hit a switch on the wall. Tiny white lights flickered to life all around the space.

"Is there anything I can help with?" Kaleb said.

"Nope, you're our guest. And I think we're about ready. I told Nic not to let you come too early, for that very reason."

Soon plates of food were being passed around amid the conversation that was as light and easy as the fan overhead. Most of it revolved around Dan's position as an architect at a prestigious firm. It explained why their home was so fastidiously designed.

If he ever had a family, maybe Dan could…

Scratch that. There was no way he was going to ask Nicola's father to design a house that he lived in with someone other than his daughter.

Except the person he'd just pictured in front of this imaginary house had been Nicola, standing outside in bare feet with a white straw hat on her head and a flowing white dress. She was cradling the swell of a baby bump and smiling.

At him.

"Kaleb?"

He glanced up and realized everyone was looking at him. "Sorry. Did I miss something?"

Margaret smiled. "No. I was just congratulating you and Nic on your upcoming arrival."

"Thank you. It was a surprise, but a good one."

And it *was* a good one. Once the shock had

worn off, he realized he was happy—in a way that felt strange and yet very right. Things were changing, and surprisingly it wasn't the disaster he'd imagined when Nic first told him about the baby.

"I guess so. Nic said she was going to wait a little longer to tell us, but a mutual friend spilled the beans."

Mutual friend. That was one way to put it. Were they unhappy that Nicola's ex wasn't the one who'd fathered her child?

He decided to let them know that he wasn't going to abandon her. "Her first prenatal exam went well. The baby had a slightly elevated heart rate…" When he glanced at Nic, she was staring at him in a way that… Okay, so he evidently wasn't supposed to have told them that. He tried to fix it. "Bill said it wasn't far out of the normal range, though. And probably due to excitement."

Or stress.

"*Bill* did her exam?" Dan chimed in this time, and lo and behold, Nicola was giving him that look again. One he had no problem reading. He'd intercepted the same kind of looks between his parents and realized they had a secret language where no words were needed.

Was that what they were doing?

"My obstetrician was doing an emergency C-section, Dad. She couldn't be there."

"How's he doing? Bill, I mean?"

Margaret spoke up. "Dan…" Her voice held a warning note.

"He's fine. We don't really talk very much anymore, for obvious reasons."

Dan evidently liked Bill. Maybe his earlier thought about them wishing Dan had fathered this child wasn't so far from the truth after all.

Kaleb cut into his steak, and as he did felt pressure against his thigh. He glanced over at Nicola and realized she'd put her leg against his. This time not to chastise him, but to re-assure him. And it did.

"So, Kaleb and I were in Central Park a little while ago and actually had to help a boy who'd gotten hurt on a hoverboard."

"Oh, wow," Margaret said. "Is he going to be okay?"

"He is, but he fell pretty hard."

"Good thing you were there." She smiled. "Nic said you're going to be involved with the baby's life. That makes us so happy."

The quick change in subject threw him for a minute, but Margaret's voice rang with a sincerity that washed away the discomfort he'd been feeling over being here.

"I wouldn't have it any other way."

"Well—" she reached out and took her husband's hand "we want you to know that you're welcome in our home anytime. Nic speaks very highly of you."

"She told me she'd vouched for me." He sent Nicola a smile that carried hidden meaning. Her leg pressed against his again, letting him know that she'd gotten it.

He liked it. This secret communication that went on between two people. He'd never done this with either of his exes or with anyone else he'd dated.

The mood was warm and festive, and Nicola's parents helped carry most of the conversation, which took the burden off of Kaleb and Nic. He could just sit back and enjoy the evening, which was a far cry from how he'd expected this night to go. He glanced over and caught Nicola laughing at something her dad had said about a client who wanted a house shaped like the international space station. "You're kidding!"

"Nope. I told him that was beyond my skill set and referred him to my least favorite competitor."

They all laughed.

Nic's eyes met his and an urge to take her hand came over him. He made a fist in his lap to keep from acting on the impulse. He'd told her the truth in his office. She was beautiful. And it wasn't just on the outside. The woman's beauty went clear down to her bones. What he'd once thought abrasive, he now realized was passion. A passion for her patients. A passion for finding out the truth.

"What?" she asked.

He realized he'd been staring at her. "Nothing."

Dan and Margaret shared a look, Dan giving her a quick wink. He wasn't sure what that was about, but the warmth in his chest spread. These two were going to make wonderful grandparents. Their love for each other was plain to see even after all these years. Much like his own parents. They seemed to be in the minority nowadays, which was one of the reasons he'd discounted marriage for so long. After striking out twice, he just assumed he didn't have it in him to stick around for the long haul, since he was the one who'd broken off both of those engagements.

But Nicola was different. She was who she seemed. No hints of subterfuge in her manner. And he'd looked for it. Expected to find it. And was dumbfounded when it wasn't there.

When she said something, he could trust that she meant it. Even the way she dealt with patients was honest. She didn't make fun of them behind their backs or show impatience. Instead, she listened. Really listened.

Just like she'd done with him.

Maybe Snowden was wrong. Hell, maybe Kaleb himself was wrong. Maybe relationships *could* weather the hard times. His own parents and Nicola's had.

They'd just needed the right partner in life.

Could it be done? Well, looking at Nicola, he wondered. Her last relationship hadn't lasted, but he'd watched her treat Bill with respect, and he'd responded in kind. He smiled. His last ex had stolen half of his furniture and made no apologies for it. And he'd been okay with it, because it meant she had cleared out of there. And the one before that? Well, her wish of having a baby had come true. A few months after they broke up. Only it hadn't been with him.

And here he was about to father a child with someone else. But he was more settled now than he'd been back then. He'd thought maybe he wasn't cut out to be a father or a husband, and yet seeing that heart beating on the ultrasound had made him realize he did. The timing just had to be right.

And the woman?

While her parents continued to talk, he used Nicola's tactic and nudged her leg with his. She smiled at him, a tiny dimple appearing at the corner of her mouth. Making her smile was a heady thing. He nudged again.

She responded back, this time using more of her upper thigh. It brushed along his, awakening nerve endings that weren't in his chest, this time.

Secret communications. Oh, yes. He liked them.

He then pressed his whole leg against hers, his foot hooking around her ankle and exerting slow pressure, until her legs parted slightly. Then he smiled at her. A smile that carried a completely different meaning from his earlier ones.

The tip of her tongue came out to moisten her lips. Then she blinked and sat upright. "I think I just heard my phone ping. I'll be right back." Pulling free, she pushed her chair away from the table and headed for the other side of the patio, where her purse was.

Hell, he guessed he'd gone too far. Of course he had. They were at her parents' house, for God's sake, and here he was trying to seduce her right there at their dinner table.

Nicola pulled out her phone and glanced at the screen. "Oh, no, Kaleb. We need to go. There's been an emergency."

That was weird. He couldn't remember being texted about a hospital emergency before. It normally came in the form of phone call.

So maybe she hadn't been trying to get away from him after all. Maybe something really was wrong at the hospital.

"Okay." He glanced at her parents. "I'm sorry to leave like this."

"It's fine. Go ahead," Dan said. "I hope you can come back again. Before the baby arrives."

He smiled. "You can count on it."

And he meant it. The evening had been entirely different than he'd imagined it.

He waited while Nicola got her stuff together, and they headed out the door.

"What's the emergency? Did they say?"

"Who's they?"

He blinked at her. "Whoever texted you."

"I didn't actually say the *text* said there was an emergency. That was spam. I get it all the time."

"What? I don't understand. What's the emergency, then?" Had she not wanted him to stay?

"The emergency was that your leg tugging on mine was starting to elicit some dangerous reactions. Those reactions were soon going to make themselves painfully known. And I don't think my parents would have appreciated me slamming you down on the table next to the bread basket and having my way with you."

Relief poured over him. "So I'm not the only one it was affecting." What had started out as something playful had taken on a life of its own. He'd heated himself up, but he hadn't been sure about her. "So what are we going to do about this so-called emergency?"

"We're going to figure out whose place is closer, and we're going to put out a fire."

He leaned over to kiss her, right there in the front yard of Nicola's childhood home. "What if I want to start a few more fires, before I put any out?"

"I know of at least one fire that is already burning. And there's only one thing that can put it out. And that's you."

CHAPTER TEN

KALEB'S HOUSE WAS CLOSER. As soon as they got through the front door, her mouth was on his, her hands grabbing at the sides of his shirt as he walked her backward. "I don't know where we're going."

"Do you need to know? I just want to enjoy the journey."

"Mmm. That sounds good."

So she let him kiss and touch and caress her as they inched their way through his home. She didn't have time to look at anything. Didn't need to look at anything. All she wanted was his hands on her.

Through a door they went and the next thing she knew, her legs were against the mattress of an unmade bed. She swallowed. He'd slept there last night, his body pressing deep into this mattress the way she wanted him to press into her. Her mouth went dry.

She was never going to forget this night.

His arms slid up her back, and he pressed her against him. "Do you trust me, Nic?"

A frisson of excitement went through her. "Yes."

His lips curved, a slow, knowing smile that touched parts of her that were already aching with need. He turned her around until she faced the bed, fitting himself against her back, that long hard part of him pushing into the softness of her behind.

She shuddered. Everything about him was a study in sensuality. He knew how to use his voice, his hands, his body, to make her writhe with need. And each time had been different. The first time, boozy and free. The second time, naughty and rushed. And this third time... Oh, God, she had a feeling he was going to take her places she'd never gone before. Things between them were changing. And he seemed okay with it. Willing to sit in the driver's seat, even.

His palms slid down her arms, until one hand reached her breasts. He cupped one, while his other hand trailed down her stomach, holding her in place while he pushed rhythmically against her. His lips were next to her ear. "Can you spend the night?"

What? How was he even forming complete sentences? Her brain was mush.

Somehow, she replied, "Yes."

"Good." He nipped her earlobe. "Because once isn't going to be enough. Not nearly enough."

The hand at her stomach slid lower, curving over her mons and exploring what he found there. Continuing to hold her against him, he released himself and guided his engorged flesh between her legs. "Close them."

Excitement bloomed when she realized what he was going to do. She squeezed her thighs together, his groan rumbling against her ear as he thrust, pleasuring himself and her, while she bit her lip until it hurt.

All too soon, he slid free.

"No..."

"Shh, I'm not done, honey. Not by a long shot."

He pulled her shirt up over her head, hands going back around to squeeze her breasts, before finding the front clasp of her bra and releasing it. He then slid the straps down her arms and let the garment fall to the floor.

When he cupped her again, her breath exited in a hiss. They were so sensitive—the nipples seeking out his palms and the decadent friction they could give.

"I love that you like this, Nic. So soft. I could touch you for hours. But first…"

He pulled back again and unbuttoned her trousers, sliding the zip and then pushing them and her undergarment down her legs. Behind her, she could hear his own clothing rustle as he discarded it.

Then he was still for a minute. But only a minute.

His hands went to hers, pulling them forward, even as he used the weight of his body to bend her torso toward the bed. She shivered, realizing what he was going to do. He pressed her hands into the mattress.

"But I want to touch you," she said.

"Next time. I promise."

His words wrapped around something inside of her and made it sing.

His fingertips skated across her shoulders, skimmed down her spine, smoothed over the curve of her backside. He pressed his lips into the middle of her back. "Spread your legs for me."

Her breath caught as she slowly walked her feet apart, the cool air in his apartment flowing over her in an intimate caress that made her moan. Then his hands were on her hips, holding her still for what she knew was coming. For what she needed to come.

He was at her entrance, slowly pushing inside, stretching her in a way that was too delicious for words. He went deep, straining into her. Like her nipples, everything he touched was unbelievably sensitive. It was like her whole body's nerve endings were tuned in to his every move…each awaiting their turn to be stroked.

He eased back and drove forward again, going just as deep, holding tight against her. She tried to increase the pace, her need rising up, but he held her still, shushing her when she made to protest. "It's okay. I need to feel you. All of you."

He wasn't touching her anywhere else, but she didn't need it. Her whole being was focused like a laser beam on that single point of contact. His movements stayed slow and deliberate. She would say lazy, except he seemed to be keeping a razor-edged level of control, pushing his limits—and hers—to the very brink.

Then his hand came around and touched her. Just a light flick. Then another, all as he held still inside of her. There were no boundaries between them. There was no need for them anymore, since she was pregnant. She felt the smooth pull, like a rubber band being stretched, further and further, waiting to be set free.

His finger tapped and released, tapped and released.

She wanted him to move inside of her. Wanted him to thrust hard and fast. But he was so very still, his breath coming in gusts against her neck, making her skin prickle.

What had been a light tap got heavier with need. The silence in the room added another layer of expectancy to what was already happening inside of her. She wanted to moan, to scream, but didn't want to break up what was happening. She realized what he was doing. He was setting a scene, readying it for the inevitable climax. Her body's nerve endings had shut down everything in her body except for one tiny set, which was shuddering a little closer with every tap.

Tap...pause. Tap...pause. Tap...pause.

She could feel herself shifting to another plane, her nipples tightening, belly tensing.

The tapping stopped. No. No! *No!* She hung there for a second, then felt the wave beginning to flicker in preparation for receding from the edge. She clawed to stay there, didn't want to leave this place. Not ever.

Then without warning, his thumb and forefinger gripped her, squeezing in quick pulsing motions that rushed her with lightning speed back toward her goal. And then she was flying over it, Kaleb's arm wrapping around her midsection to hold her in place, when she tried to pump. He kept her there, her mind bending as wave after wave of pleasure tore through her. Still motionless, Kaleb suddenly groaned against her ear and she realized he was climaxing without even needing to move.

I want to feel you.

God. Literally that's what he'd done.

He kissed her neck. Nipped her shoulder. Traced her upper back with his tongue. He took a deep breath and then let it blow out. "Thank you."

He was thanking *her*? He was the one who'd done all the work.

"I don't know what you just did to me. But I don't think I'm ever going to recover."

He suddenly tipped her face to look at her. "Are you okay?"

Oh! He thought he'd hurt her. "No. I meant, I have never experienced anything like that in my life. It was…" She chuckled. "There are no words."

"Mmm. Same here." He kissed her lips, then pulled free. "But we have a lot more fires to deal with before the night is over."

He was right. It was just after midnight, and every fiber of her being was satiated. She was bone-jarringly tired. And happy. And… all kinds of other things.

Kaleb leaned back against the pillows, his hands behind his head.

The other two times she'd been with him, things had been rushed and hurried. She'd never gotten to see the "aftermath Kaleb." As she studied him, she liked what she saw. Wouldn't mind seeing a whole lot more of this side of him in the future.

But was that what he wanted? She wasn't sure.

She turned onto her side and propped herself on her elbow to get a better look. "I vote we don't tell my parents why we needed to leave their house so quickly tonight."

"I think your dad might hunt me down and throw my carcass on his grill. Medium on the left, well-done on the right."

She laughed. "Are you worried?"

"It depends on whether you'll vouch for me if and when he does."

"Always."

As soon as she said the word, Kaleb rolled over, taking her with him. His forearms bracketing her face, he ran his fingertips over her cheeks and slid down to her lips. "Always?"

"Yes." There was something about the way he said that word that made her shiver.

He kissed her. A long slow kiss that seemed to go on forever. Despite how tired she was, her body flickered back to life.

"I think your parents would like to see us married."

"Mmm…probably. But they'll get used to it the way it is."

"Maybe we should."

His statement came out of nowhere, shocking her. "Should what?"

"Get married?"

"Are you serious? Why?"

There'd been nothing to ever suggest he wanted to get married. In fact, they'd both been pretty adamant that they didn't.

"Why not? It would make everything so much easier."

"What things? You mean the baby?"

"The baby. The situation with your parents. With my parents. Our coworkers. It would take care of all the awkward explanations. People have married for worse reasons."

Her eyes widened. Maybe "they" did, but she didn't. And the fact that he was willing to uproot his life—change everything—just to make those "awkward explanations" easier to handle was horrifying. Unimaginable.

For one thing, her parents would see through the ruse in no time. Pretending to not know him was one thing. But to pretend they loved each other in public, while in private they both knew it was a lie, that in reality… God!

And he was okay with that?

Well, she wasn't. Wasn't willing to put their baby through the eventual meltdown that was bound to happen over time, when

Kaleb realized he couldn't keep up the charade anymore. When he eventually walked out on them...

The fear she'd had right after she realized she was pregnant came back to haunt her. That thought that he might want to marry her just for the sake of the baby. Back then she'd blurted out that she had no intention of getting married. He'd agreed with her at the time. And yet here he was, knocking on her door and saying the complete opposite.

There were worse reasons, he'd said.

Except she couldn't imagine anything worse than what he'd just offered her. A marriage of convenience. Of necessity, to avoid awkwardness.

She closed her eyes. She'd always thought if she eventually married, it would be the real deal. It would be because someone loved her. That they couldn't imagine life without her. But Kaleb felt none of those things.

Even Bill had loved her for...her.

In his office, she thought of how sexy Kaleb was, how he could end up being a real heartbreaker, but that he hadn't broken her heart.

She was wrong. Because he just had. She

recoiled away as a terrible realization swept over her, swamping her and pressing her flat. "Absolutely not."

"Why? Give me one good reason why it wouldn't make life easier for both of us. For the baby."

Why? Because as she'd been lying here staring up at him, the truth had dawned on her. A truth so tragic that it made what he'd just said to her feel obscene.

Somewhere during the ten weeks they'd known each other, an astounding thing had been growing inside of her. Something that had nothing to do with the baby.

And everything to do with love.

She loved him.

She wasn't sure exactly when or where it had happened, but it had.

He was right. Marrying her would make everything easier. Would make everyone happier.

Everyone except for...her.

Oh, no—*please*, no.

And explaining to him her reasons for turning him down was not an option. She couldn't do it. And she definitely couldn't stay while he continued to list all the reasons why she should say yes.

Because she couldn't. Couldn't say yes.

Not now. Not ever.

Those two phrases repeated over and over in her head until she thought she might vomit.

"I… I'll, um… I'll let you know." She would. But not right now. Not when the burning behind her eyes was about a minute away from turning into a very real flood.

Right now, all she wanted or needed was to escape. To get away before he realized she'd just become the biggest fool on the face of the planet: a woman who'd fallen for a man who only wanted to marry her to make things easy.

Well, it wouldn't. They would make her life hell on earth. Because he was bound to find out the truth, and when he did…

She pushed him off of her and sat up, dragging the sheet around her. "I need to get going. I have an early shift and Danvers wants to run another case by me."

Kaleb frowned, then levered himself up, too. "Are you okay?"

The question almost broke her in two. It was the exact question he'd asked her after they made love tonight. And her answer now was the polar opposite of what it had been then.

"I'm fine. I—I had a good time tonight, thank you. And thanks for coming to my parents' for dinner. See you tomorrow?" No, he wouldn't, but she was not going to let him know about the plan that had just crystalized in her head—a plan that was based solely on a survival instinct she didn't realize she had. Emotional survival rather than physical.

"Do you want me to drive you home?"

"No, my car is here. It'll be easier in the morning if it's at my house."

She hopped out of bed and started dragging on her clothes, trying not to make it look like she was hurrying, but with the way her hands were shaking, it was hard. She threw him a smile just to make sure he didn't follow her outside. "We'll sort out appointments and so forth sometime next week."

"Okay." He got out of bed and caught her wrist. "Are you sure you're okay, Nic?"

"Yes. Just exhausted." She gave a short laugh. "You wore me out."

The correct phrase would have been that

she was emotionally wrung out, but that might have made him ask more questions.

"Stay the night, then. You said you would."

"No." She casually lifted her hand to her head to force him to release his grip. She then dragged her fingers through her hair as if straightening it, when really, she didn't care how she looked. "I don't have a change of clothes here, and it'll be so much easier to just…" Too late, she realized she'd parroted his earlier words back to him. It wouldn't be easier. Nothing would be easier for a long, long time.

She could figure everything with the baby out later, but right now, she just needed to get out.

"Okay. Call me to let me know you made it home."

No way was she doing that. "I'll let you know." She'd send him a one-word text, and that was it.

She grabbed her handbag and headed for the front door, just hoping she could make it to her car and onto the street before she broke down.

And then tomorrow, once she'd composed

herself, she was going to put her plan into action. Before anyone—especially Kaleb—realized what was happening.

CHAPTER ELEVEN

ALL HE HAD was a text. One saying that while he could be in the baby's life, Nicola didn't want to marry him. Didn't even want them to continue seeing each other. He'd tried calling her and texting her back, but he'd gotten no response.

And coming out of Harvey Smith's office two days later, he felt shell-shocked. She was gone. Back to her old hospital without saying a word to him as to why.

According to Harvey, she wanted to try to work at both hospitals, consulting at NYC Memorial only when there was a specific case that needed her input. And most of those consultations would happen via a telemedicine link. She wouldn't even need to physically come to the hospital.

The administrator had been fine with that, telling her if she changed her mind or if her caseload got to be too heavy to let him know, and they'd put her back on NYC Memorial's schedule.

What on earth had brought this on? They'd had a sexy evening that she'd been totally into, after leaving her parents' house. Hell, it had been her idea to go back to his place and make love.

She'd been absolutely fine.

Until he mentioned marriage. And then she was up and out of there in a flash. It was almost like she'd been expecting him to ask and was already poised to turn him down. Which she had. In no uncertain terms. Except at the very end, she'd said she would think about it. He guessed she had. And her answer was still no.

His thought after she'd left his apartment was "well, at least she didn't take my furniture." But it had been in a funny sense. He hadn't seriously thought she was walking out of his life for good. Her text had said he could be part of his baby's life, but she hadn't said exactly what that would look like.

His question of marriage had been half joking, but if she'd said yes, he would have gone through with it. He really had thought maybe they could make a go of it.

The one thing missing had been love. But he'd gone the love route twice before and had flamed out. This time, he'd thought if he could go into it with more thought and build it on something other than fickle emotion, it might work. He cared about her. And he'd been pretty sure—until that text—that she might care about him, as well.

Well, hell. Maybe she'd just saved him from one more failed relationship. He should thank Snowden for suggesting they make that toast.

He'd give Nicola a week or so and then try to approach her about the part he was going to play in his child's life. She didn't want to get married? Fine. But he hadn't changed his mind about wanting to be a father in a very real sense of the word.

Okay, he'd give it a week. And then he'd try to call again, and if that failed, he was going to march over to Grace Central and have it out with her in person. If she didn't have him thrown off the property the way she'd thrown him out of her life.

Snow met him at the bar. Their bar. His and Nicola's, where it had all begun. She still hadn't answered his calls, and now he had a decision to make. Over a drink, he told his old friend what had transpired in clinical terms, letting him know that he was going to be a father.

"I knew something was up. I just didn't know what. For supposedly just having met her when Harvey introduced you, you two seemed to know each other a little more than I would have expected. But I had no idea, she was already pregnant."

"I didn't know, either. At least not then. She took a pregnancy test a week or so after you saw us, and it came back positive."

"So if she agreed that you could be a part of the baby's life, and you met her parents, what happened?"

"I don't know. I said her parents probably wanted us to get married and suggested that maybe it wasn't such a bad idea. She took off like a bat out of hell."

"You did what?"

"Yeah. I didn't realize I was that bad of a catch."

"Exactly what reason did you give her for wanting to get married?"

Kaleb took a drink of his beer, wiping the foam from his mouth with the back of his hand. "I said it would make everything easier."

"Easier." Snow laughed. "Man, no wonder you were willing to make that toast. You wouldn't know how to catch a girl if she was placed on your hook."

"I caught two of them just fine, thank you very much. They just weren't what I was looking for."

Snow smiled and leaned forward, thumping his untouched whiskey glass on the bar. "And just what were you looking for, Kaleb? Something that would make everything easier?"

"No, of course not. I was looking for lov…" He swallowed. Damn. No wonder she'd taken off. No wonder she'd sent him a text that had basically said thanks, but no thanks.

"Right. And don't you think this girl—Nicola—might have been looking for the same thing? Not a man who thought marrying her would make everything easier. For him."

"Hell. I thought I was playing it smart this time. Thinking it through without letting my heart or my—" his eyes fell to his lap before coming back up "—lead me around."

"And that, my friend, is the biggest mistake of them all. Not that I'm looking for love anytime soon. Whether or not you choose to,

I'm sticking to my vow." He pushed his glass around the polished surface of the bar. "I only have one question."

"What's that?"

"If you married this girl, would you be marrying her for love? Or for the convenience of it?"

Kaleb frowned. "I'm not sure I under—" Suddenly he got it. Realized how far off base he'd been in asking her that question. How insulting it had probably sounded. And it had been a lie. Marrying her wouldn't make things easier.

His throat closed up as he ran through all the things he and Nic had shared in such a short period of time: Collaborated at work. Laughed over drinks. Stood over a baby's bed as he recovered from surgery. Made love like there was no tomorrow.

And he realized his answer to Snow's question was yes. He would have been marrying Nicola for all the right reasons. He just hadn't understood it at the time.

He loved the woman.

"Yeah. You're right. And I'm a damn fool."

"Then forget about our toast and go find the woman and tell her you're not marrying her to make your life easier. In fact, it's about to get a hell of a lot harder. But whatever you do, don't leave out *why* you want to marry her. If that doesn't change things, call me, and we'll go out and get roaring drunk. But if it does…then don't call me until you set a date."

He clapped Kaleb on the back. "Good luck, old friend."

"Thanks. Thanks for everything. Including that toast. Because it led me right to where I needed to be." And with that, Kaleb climbed off his barstool and headed for the door. He knew exactly what he needed to do.

CHAPTER TWELVE

Nicola stared at her computer screen without really seeing it. So far she'd only been over to NYC Memorial two times in the last three weeks. And both of those times, she'd snuck in and out by doors she didn't usually use. It felt stupid, but seeing Kaleb under these circumstances would be unbearable.

She hadn't been able to believe he'd asked to marry her because of the baby. Because of their parents.

To be fair, she hadn't asked him if he loved her. But they say if you have to ask…

Who are "they"? And what kind of data are "they" using to come to that conclusion?

Conclusion.

How did someone come to a conclusion?

Well, she knew how *she* normally did. And it wasn't by sitting around and moping and wishing things were different.

So why not do what she was good at? What she'd trained herself to do?

Taking out her sketchbook, she opened it to the first blank page. Then she got to work, drawing her boxes and meticulously labeling each of them. Then using the data from things she knew to be true, she began to draw her lines. Phrases that were said. Experiences that were had. Each thing made her line slide to one of two possible conclusions at the bottom of her page.

She touched her belly when it growled. Someone was getting hungry. "I know, sweetie. But there's just something I have to do first."

Tapping her pen on her chin, she went day by day, remembering little things. It wouldn't be an exact diagnosis because there was no blood test known to man that could measure what she was looking for. No MRI that could find and pinpoint the truth. This would be purely circumstantial evidence that wouldn't hold up in any court of law. But it would be enough to draw an inference from.

Two more lines trailed down to their spots on the chart. Three more. Ten. And an hour later, when she was done, she tallied them up and wrote her conclusion—a single word—at the very bottom of her page and underlined it three times.

Then she closed her sketchbook and held it tight to her chest, fear and hope warring with each other. Until one of them won out. She climbed to her feet in her little work area and tidied up her desk…straightened her chair. If she was right, this would be the last time she would sit here.

And if she was wrong?

Well, she wasn't handing in her notice—again—quite yet.

Turning around so that she could walk to the exit, she staggered to a stop when she spotted someone striding toward her. A phantom who had haunted her days and nights ever since she'd walked out of his house. The person she'd been getting ready to go see.

"Kaleb?"

He'd called her repeatedly, but she hadn't been able to bring herself to answer. Not until this very moment.

He approached her. "Hey."

"Hey."

"I've been trying to reach you."

"I know."

God, why did they have to go through all of this stupid small talk in order to get to what was really important. What would make or break the next seven months of her pregnancy.

He took a step closer, seeming encouraged when she didn't walk away from him. "Is there somewhere we can go to talk?"

"Yes. Let's go to the courtyard out back." Leading the way to an area that was more of a paved outdoor faculty lounge than a garden, she found a table at the farthest side of the small space, and laid her sketchbook on top of the melamine surface.

"Nic. I owe you an apology. A big one."

"You do?"

He nodded, starting to reach for her hand before evidently thinking better of it. "I never should have asked you to marry me the last night we were together."

Shock went through her system. And horror. Maybe she'd been wrong. Maybe she should tear that page out of her book and put it through the shredder before he or anyone else saw it. "You shouldn't have?"

"No. Not until I understood what was really driving the question."

She pulled air into her lungs in rhythmic intervals so she wouldn't pass out. "And you think you understand it now?"

"I know I do. And I hope you'll hear me out." This time, he did take her hand, lacing his fingers through hers. "I love you, Nic. The way I've never loved anyone before."

She blinked. Tried to process what he'd just said.

"But you said… You told me you wanted to marry me for all that other stuff. Stuff that has nothing to do with love."

"I know." He let out a sigh. "I'd been down that road—meaning love—a couple of times before, and it always ended disastrously. I thought if I could just be analytical about it this time and give it a name *other* than love, then maybe it would work. Because I desperately wanted it to work, Nic. I still do."

"You do?" Shock turned to laughter, the sound pealing forth until tears streamed down her face, even as he tried to scoot his chair around to console her. She shook him off with a hiccup. "Oh, God, Kaleb. Do you want to see what name I came up with when I tried to be all analytical about it?"

"I'm not sure at this point."

She riffled through her sketchbook until she came up with the right graph and flipped it open so he could see. "Look."

Watching as he worked his way across the page, slowly moving down and reading the words, box by box. Finally, when he'd studied it for what seemed like hours, his fingers traced the lines down to their final resting places and the underlined conclusion.

"Love." His gaze came up and speared her. "You love me?"

"I didn't do the graph to figure out how *I* felt. Read the name at the top."

He looked at where she pointed. "It's my name."

"Yes. I already knew what my feelings were, but I didn't know about you. And your marriage question that night wandered around so much, that it made me wonder if the word you were so afraid of using lay smack-dab in the center." She squeezed his hand. "I was right. Wasn't I?"

"You were. Hell. I can't believe I put both of us through that. But I thought if I said the word *love*, I might jinx it, just like I did those other times."

"You didn't jinx it. Those other times just

weren't meant to be. But I think we are. I think what you sensed about my parents was right, as well. They saw it before even we did."

He leaned his cheek against hers, breathing deeply. "Don't throw that page away, Nicola. I want to keep it. Frame it. I want it on the wall in our bedroom so that through the bad times and the good, we'll see those lines leading from where we were to the spot we both want to be." He tapped the word she'd written in the box at the bottom. "Love. That's where I want to stay. With you. Forever."

She cupped his face and looked into his eyes. "I do, too, Kaleb. I never want to step outside of that box. But if either of us does, all we need to do is follow those lines, until they lead us back to this place. Back to where we belong. Those lines will lead us all the way home."

* * * * *

*Look out for the next story in the
New York Bachelor's Club duet*

The Trouble with the Tempting Doc

*And if you enjoyed this story, check out
these other great reads from Tina Beckett*

It Started with a Winter Kiss
Risking it All for the Children's Doc
One Hot Night with Dr. Cardoza

All available now!